God Rest Ye Merry Spinster

Also by

Rebecca Connolly

The Arrangements:

An Arrangement of Sorts

Married to the Marquess

Secrets of a Spinster

The Dangers of Doing Good

The Burdens of a Bachelor

A Bride Worth Taking

A Wager Worth Making

A Gerrard Family Christmas

The Spinster Chronicles:

The Merry Lives of Spinsters

The Spinster and I

Spinster and Spice

My Fair Spinster

Coming Soon

What a Spinster Wants

God Rest Ye Merry Spinster

REBECCA CONNOLLY

Phase Publishing, LLC
Seattle

Cover art by Tugboat Design
http://www.tugboatdesign.net

Phase Publishing, LLC first paperback edition
December 2019

ISBN 978-1-943048-98-4
Library of Congress Control Number 2019918808

Cataloging-in-Publication Data on file.

Acknowledgements

To Amy Grant for being the female vocalist of Christmas in my life. It just wouldn't be Christmas without you, and that's the truth.

And to peppermint bark for being the most beautiful treat I never fail to forget I love until Christmas season rolls around.

Prologue

London, 1816

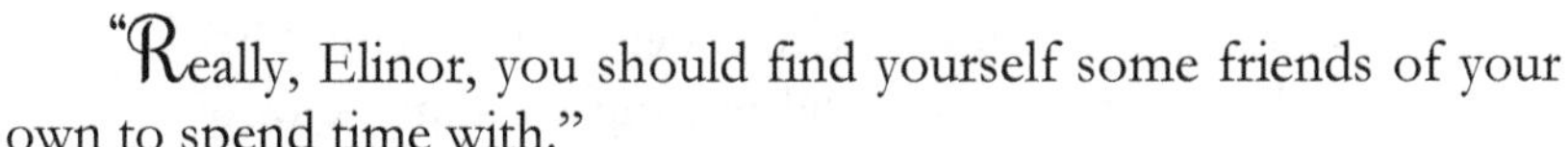

"Really, Elinor, you should find yourself some friends of your own to spend time with."

"I *have* friends, Emma, and they all wish to spend their time speaking of courtship and gentlemen and weddings, though none of them have understandings or beaux. It's the silliest bunch of tittle-tattle you've ever heard, and I quite tire of it."

"So, you'd rather spend your time with a group of spinsters who speak of nothing of the kind, is that it?"

"Yes, I rather think I would."

"Well, you can't. You're barely seventeen."

"You have to let me come with you. Mama insisted you get me out of the house today, remember? You're charged with my care. How can you care for me when I'm not in your presence or your immediate vicinity?"

There was a moment of hesitation, conflict dancing across features, and then resignation.

Elinor Asheley knew she had won then. Her sister would *have* to take her to the Spinsters meeting now. She'd been trying to get access for an entire year, ever since she'd first discovered just what her sister and her friends were capable of. She hadn't cared at all when they'd only been meeting and occasionally went about London together, but when they had somehow managed to get a paper circulated to all of London, she had grown curious. When she'd managed to snag a copy for herself and read it, which her mother had prevented for some reason or other, she had known in an instant that she must be part of them.

She'd never thought of marriage or romance or the like. She did not care about courtship, and she was desperately tired of the wasteful young men she had seen come and go in Society. Surely young ladies deserved better, and if nothing else, the Spinsters could help encourage them in such straits.

Some ladies did wish to marry, though Elinor had never seen any reason to. They should be able to marry the best quality of men, if such a thing existed, and someone ought to ensure that such men, whoever they were, could be easily identified somehow.

Why, there could even be a collection of information about appropriate suitors with details of their natures and their prospects and the like. What a useful and wise endeavor that would be!

And with that, those who did not meet the mark would never have a chance of ensnaring young women who were too naive or too ignorant to understand the dangers they were putting themselves in.

Whoever engaged in such a work would surely be a champion of virtue and feminine rights.

But, if nothing else, she could be part of a paper and a cause that would be far more exciting and invigorating than sitting around at home mucking up needlework or plunking away at the pianoforte.

That would also suit.

"Well," Emma sighed as she tied her bonnet ribbons over her fair curls, still less than pleased to be toting Elinor along with her, "shall we go? I don't know what Charlotte and the others will make of it, but I'll assure them it will not be a regular occurrence."

"Of course," Elinor demurred with a sly smile as she fetched her own bonnet. "Not at all regular."

Chapter One

There is nothing like family at the holidays. Truly. Nothing at all.

-The Spinster Chronicles, 4 December 1819

Christmas at Deilingh was at once the best and worst time of her life.

It would be one thing if the sprawling, near-crumbling estate contained only her siblings and her parents, and the accompanying spouses and children, naturally. It was quite another when the twenty-seven bedrooms were entirely filled with cousins, cousins by marriage, aunts, uncles, two great-aunts, and Uncle Dough, though no one was quite sure how he fit into the family schematic.

Elinor had tried to have her father explain to her why everybody retreated to Deilingh for Christmas in Derbyshire when the estate belonged to her uncle Howard, her father's eldest brother, who wasn't even in England this year, but it was no use. It had been a longstanding Asheley tradition to all gather together for Christmas at Deilingh, and so they continued to do so.

Uncle Howard might have been the most fortunate member of the family, as he had left for Canada in the early autumn to look into some intriguing investment opportunities, whatever that meant, and had opted to remain there until spring. The house, therefore, and its running, went to Elinor's father, as Uncle Howard only had daughters, and six of them at that.

All of whom were here with their husbands.

Add to that her aunt Catherine, her husband Mr. Jones, and their three daughters, none of whom were married; her father's cousin, Mr. Perry, who was the stodgiest clergyman known to man, his wife Hortensia, who looked as one might expect a Hortensia to look, and their two homely yet eligible sons, Walter and Hubert; Uncle James with his very young second wife Anna and his three daughters from his first marriage, two with burly husbands and impressively vocal children, as well as the four children from the second marriage, who were the spawn of the devil himself.

Also, her great-aunt Julie and her great-aunt Beatrice, who were both hard of hearing when it suited them, and had taken up the idea that being elderly gave them license to do and say as they pleased without consequence, as evidenced by their consuming the entire stock of port last Christmas and sliding down the bannisters of the great stairs, then lining up every girl in the family and telling them exactly what was wrong with their form, figure, or finishing, and ending with falling into a snoring, babbling sleep in front of the Yule log, which had seemed a dreadful risk to the entire house in general, given the amount of alcohol in and around their persons.

There were two or three other significant persons, aside from Uncle Dough, she was sure, but she really could not bear to go through the list again. Her own family seemed perfectly tame by comparison, and that was a terrible statement to make.

It was madness. Complete and utter madness, there was no other way to describe it.

And yet, every year, she found herself laughing, smiling, and generally admiring the fact that her perfectly respectable family could be filled to the brim with such extraordinary characters. No one quite understood her cousins the way they all did, and even they did not understand them half of the time. Nothing Great-Aunt Julie or Beatrice could say really bothered the lot of them anymore, and everyone knew full well not to go near Mr. Perry for any religious reasons.

It was the same thing every year, dreading being cooped away at Deilingh and then finding the dread growing less and less as the usual activities and traditions took place. There was some comfort in the fact that nothing ever really changed between them, no matter what might have gone on throughout the year or during the Season. Christmas at Deilingh remained as it ever had.

Somehow, she tended to forget that every year.

Along with the recollection that when all gathered together, everyone expressed their opinion about everything. Such as the idea that Elinor was doing herself no favors by cavorting about with the Spinsters in London, and she was ruining her chances for marriage.

Which was the current topic of conversation.

"It's just not sensible, Elinor," her cousin Joan told her as she picked up her second, or perhaps third, child from the floor. "You'll frighten off any man who might wish to try for you."

"Indeed," Cousin Mary added, tugging a needle and thread through her abysmal attempt at embroidery. "What a terrifying prospect for a man. The Spinsters would surely ward them off."

"Your sister had the sense to leave them," Cousin Millie pointed out absently as she sorted through various pieces of Christmas music. "And the moment she did, there was Mr. Partlowe, and now she is a wife and mother, and happy as a lark."

Elinor smiled tightly, smoothly pressing her own needle and thread into the handkerchief she was to give her father on Christmas Day. "Are larks actually happy birds, I wonder?" she mused to herself, keeping her tone mild. She looked towards her bluestocking cousin at the far side of the room. "Barbara, are larks considered jovial in the world of ornithology?"

Barbara looked up from her pile of books, her spectacles blinking in an appropriately owlish manner. "I don't believe so… Their song is considered cheerful, but as to the birds themselves, I confess ignorance. I don't believe there is any particular temperament considered in the study of birds, is that significant?"

"It ought to be," Elinor's sister Elizabeth muttered beside her, widening her eyes for effect as she sorted ribbons. "If Emma is compared to a lark, one would wish to know the manner of larks, would one not?"

Elinor bit back a snort, nudging her sister a little.

"What was that, E?" Joan asked with some distraction, as her child was now tugging at her lace cap rather insistently.

Elizabeth smiled with perfection. "I was only saying that Emma was fortunate enough to meet Partlowe *while* being with the Spinsters, Joan. She left them after the marriage, if I am not mistaken."

Joan shared a look with her sister Millie, then shook her head at them. "No, I am sure you're wrong. I am quite sure you are."

"Silly me," Elizabeth grumbled to Elinor, pretending to match a ribbon to her thread. "I must be mistaken, of course, I was only there for the whole of it…"

"Shh," Elinor scolded softly, her affection for her sister growing stronger by the moment.

"Elinor isn't getting married," her youngest sister Ellen rang out with a devious edge. "She's sworn against it."

The entire room gasped, even Barbara, who was nigh on thirty herself and could not speak to men she was not related to without molting in parts. Elinor hissed through her teeth as she glared at Ellen, who knew full well she would be in for it later.

"That cannot be so," Cousin Letitia breathed, horrified at such an idea. "Your life would be over."

"Was it an earnest vow?" Fredericka asked as she crossed herself three times. "Surely it was not made in a church."

Elinor looked up at the delicate moldings of the faded ceiling above her. "No, I am no apostate, nor am I inclined to making public vows. I am inclined to be a spinster due to the lack of incentive to marry, and the lack of appealing prospects in the potential candidates. I am quite satisfied that my soul is safe from eternal damnation, given the Lord himself would not object to a young woman wanting the best husband possible for her life and not just any man who might ask."

The silence of the room seemed to refute her logic, but she was quite used to that particular notion.

"Have you refused anyone?" her cousin Lavinia asked with hesitation, the faded, nondescript shade of her hair even more flat in the faint winter light.

Elinor shook her head. "No, cousin. No one has asked."

There was a general sigh that irritated her, but she said nothing in response to it.

"You'll feel differently when someone does ask you," Mary assured her. "I did."

"So did I," Joan replied with fervent nods. "Very much so."

"Oh, good," Elinor said to no one in particular. "Something to look forward to, then."

Elizabeth snickered. "Shall we begin parading suitors to see how it feels to be asked?"

Elinor shrugged once. "Why not? It seems that's all that is necessary to change my mind."

"And one never knows," Letitia remarked with a wry smirk that did not suit her plain features, "there are bound to be several balls of mistletoe hanging about Deilingh in the next few days."

The others seemed to giggle and nod at that, but Elinor had no such inklings. "I am related to everybody currently in the house, cousin," she retorted, kindly refraining from adding that this particular cousin she was addressing did not have a husband either and was far and away more a spinster than she.

"Cousins marry all the time," she shot back, completely unperturbed. "And your father is bound to invite local families. It is tradition."

"Speaking of mistletoe," Elizabeth said quickly, seizing Elinor's arm and forcing her up, "we did promise to help Emma and Mr. Partlowe with assembling the greenery so that it might be ready for Christmas Eve. Do excuse us. Ellen, come."

Ellen did so with remarkable obedience, a thing unheard of in her young life, and she flocked to Elizabeth's side as they left the room.

"Why did I have to come?" the girl hissed. "I didn't promise."

"None of us did, you ninny," Elizabeth replied. "I don't trust you in that room unsupervised, and they were about to eat Elinor alive. Thank God everyone thinks seventeen too young for a husband in there, or I would be lumped in."

"I wouldn't," Ellen said with a sniff. "I am still a child to everyone, though I am fifteen."

Elinor rolled her eyes, wondering if this was how Charlotte felt with her on a regular basis. "Fifteen *is* a child, Elle. The only wives of fifteen are scandalous ones and no one likes a ruined woman, married or not."

Ellen ignored her. "Was it just me," she began, "or was Letitia saying she was not above marrying a cousin?"

"She was indeed," Elizabeth confirmed, shuddering and making a face. "Given the only eligible cousins in the house are Walter and Rupert, I'm surprised she could stomach the admission. What are we, desperate royals?"

"Royals marry cousins?" Ellen gasped.

"Loads of people marry cousins," Elinor groaned, swatting the air in front of her sister impatiently. "The royals are simply more public about it."

"Would you marry one of them?"

"Not if we were the only two people on earth and civilization depended on it. Humans could die out, for all I care. I'd have a clear conscience."

Elizabeth shook her head, brow furrowed. "Local families, she said. Does she think we've had new neighbors in the last fifteen years? Or do you think she'd actually consider Lord Clarksdale?"

"Lord save us," Ellen whispered, pressing her hands into praying motion. "That would make him related to us, and I'd never bear the shame."

"There's always Phillip Drew," Elinor remarked with a coy smile. "He's closer in age."

"And three times the size!" Elizabeth laughed. "Not to mention constantly intoxicated."

"And poor," Ellen broke in, as though that were the worst part of it.

All three nodded, for it truly might have been.

"Perhaps the Spinsters should put their talents to work on Letitia, Elinor," Elizabeth suggested with a sly smile. "You have plenty of research to find her someone worth having."

Elinor gave her younger sister a quelling look. "If the woman is mad enough to actually consider Rupert and Walter eligible candidates, I have no hesitation whatsoever in letting her fend for herself. I had no idea she was so desperate. Lavinia isn't, and you know Lucinda isn't."

Ellen snorted loudly. "Lucinda doesn't care about anything but perfecting her tarts and pies. Who in their right minds *wants* to be a cook when they are gently born and bred?"

"She's trying to convince her parents to let her move to Paris," Elizabeth said, lowering her voice. "She wants to study their food, for some reason."

"With all the trouble France has caused of late?" Elinor scoffed and shook her head. "It's possibly the worst place in the world she could wish to be, but perhaps the food is worth almost certain death."

"I doubt that," Ellen muttered. "It's French."

"This seems promising. Where are my passel of little sisters off to?"

They all turned towards the stairs they had just passed, looking up at their lone brother, Edmund, coming down towards them. It struck Elinor at that moment that, of all the Asheley children, Edmund was the only one to have inherited their father's dark eyes. They all looked unnervingly similar in every other respect, though the girls were certainly distinct enough to tell apart, and they'd all heard the comments enough to have memorized responses for each.

Edmund approached them, his tall, lanky form moving with the same careless ease it always had done, and he grinned broadly, as he usually did. "Well?"

"We're escaping the cousins," Ellen informed him bluntly. "They were trying to marry off Elinor."

"You started it," Elizabeth shot back.

"Did not. I merely added context."

Edmund glanced at Elinor, and she rolled her eyes, which he echoed. "Lovely, Ella-belle. So helpful, I'm sure. Sister clearly appreciated your efforts."

"So much," Elinor remarked with the dryness of the Sahara. She sighed and eyed her brother, who was clearly preparing for a ride. "Going somewhere?"

He shook his head. "Just out. Trying to escape cousins myself. Walter and Rupert seek to bring me into the fold of the church, and only half of the cousin husbands are sportsmen. Better to get a ride in before the snow gets any worse."

"Isn't there a hunt?" Elizabeth asked, propping one hand on her hip. "There's always a hunt, and the snow isn't treacherous. It's Derbyshire, not Scotland."

Edmund shrugged. "The hunt is not the same as a true ride, E. I never gallop there, and I do on a ride. Besides, Simms was saying the roads are growing nigh impassable both north and south. Mud and ice and snow, and carriages have been struggling. A single rider would be fine, but…" He smiled in a would-be eager manner. "Good thing all our blessed relations have arrived, isn't it?"

"Huzzah," the girls all responded in the same flat tone.

"Hmm," hummed a familiar voice from the drawing room nearest them. "Why do I always grow suspicious when my children gather together?"

Elinor chuckled as she looked over at her mother, standing in the doorway, arms cradling a sleeping baby. "I haven't the faintest idea, Mama. We're all so innocent."

"Is that what you call it?" she replied. "Interesting." She shifted her gaze to her son. "Edmund, you'd best leave now, I know your father and James will want you to assist them this afternoon. Girls, Emma and Partlowe could use your help with the mistletoe and greenery. They're encamped in the blue room with Alice and Anna, and I've just sent Hannah, as well."

"Does anyone else wonder how Uncle James manages with Anna as his wife and Hannah as his daughter?" Ellen asked as they all did as their mother bid. "So very similar."

Elinor gave her sister a bemused look. "They don't live together, Elle. Hannah and Mr. Layton live in Bath."

"Even so…"

Elizabeth huffed, ever the impatient one. "One could say the same thing about our family. Ellen and Elinor? Could be quite confusing."

Ellen's brow furrowed with surprisingly deep crevices. "But it isn't. That's quite clear."

"Why do I bother?" Elizabeth asked Elinor, eyes widening yet again. "Why?"

"I haven't the faintest idea."

Somehow, it seemed that the warmth of being with her cousins and other relations had yet to descend upon her. For the moment, she was still slightly disgruntled and wondering how long they were going to have to remain so completely surrounded by family and so utterly removed from anything resembling Society. Although both

Louisa and Martha had managed to marry into the peerage, and Lord Winthrop *had* said his brother John might arrive for Christmas. And he might bring friends.

Letitia might get her husband after all.

But how exactly she would manage to accomplish that when the house was overrun with children at any given time was beyond comprehension.

A series of successive shrieks from above them emphasized that point rather soundly, and Elinor bit back another sigh. She didn't mind children. Quite the opposite. In fact, she would much rather have been up in one of the nurseries playing with the children. They'd all be permitted down with the adults this afternoon until dinner, and it would be a blessed relief. None of them cared if Elinor ever married or not, and not one of them thought her association with the Spinsters ought to be commented on.

She might even be able to slip away during the chaos of the children joining them and get an article or two written for the Chronicles. It was always a bit difficult to manage the newssheet during the winter, and particularly around the holidays, but none of them had seemed to mind yet, and somehow, it always worked out well enough.

If she thought about it long enough, she might be able to submit articles about Christmas itself, or removal to the country for winter. Or even the burden of extended family.

Surely there were several people who could relate with that particular trial.

But her mother was most particular about Elinor's writing time during family occasions. Something about seclusion and making the most of the limited time they all had together; Elinor hadn't listened attentively enough to actually capture the full speech. The meaning was clear enough.

Never mind that there was nothing limited about two full weeks, sometimes three, with everyone remotely connected to them via her father's bloodlines.

She'd have to sneak time before bed at night. And she could take mental notes throughout the day. She'd have to protect identities, of course, and alter quotes enough to avoid being blatant in the retelling.

It would not do to offend her entire family, especially since she generally liked them.

Generally.

And there was the possibility that no one would find her stories as amusing as she did. Some things required years and years of context for the true scope to be appreciated, and without knowing the persons she would be describing, there would undoubtedly be something missing in the retelling.

So perhaps it would be best if she left it to something generic and relatable rather than the peculiar extremes she was used to.

Not nearly as amusing, but infinitely more sensible.

She snorted to herself. Sensible. When had she become that?

They neared the blue room only for a commotion to be heard from the front of the house. Curious, they altered course to move towards the entry hall instead, the sounds of male voices growing louder by the minute.

"Did the cousin husbands venture out this morning?" Elinor wondered aloud.

"I don't believe so," Elizabeth replied. "Lord Winthrop's brother? And several friends?"

Ellen skipped like a child for a few paces. "Someone tell Letitia!"

They burst into helpless giggles and Elinor pushed back a stray lock of her fair hair, tugging her shawl more tightly about her as they neared the cool air from the wintery day.

"Come in, come in, one and all are welcome. Plenty of room, plenty indeed."

Elinor raised a brow at her father's cheerful boast, smiling slightly. Room they had, but plenty of it, they did not. Still, there was no dampening her father's generosity and spirit.

She stopped, and her sisters along with her, and watched as her slightly rotund father gestured and waved, bustling in with what had to be six men, and her uncle James. The slick surface of her father's balding head reflected the light of the day a bit, his hat being used to emphasize his broad gesturing.

"Sally! Marie! Hopkins, where the devil is everyone?" her father called. He caught sight of Elinor and her sisters, who all waved at him in amusement.

His face broke into a beaming grin. "Hark, my herald angels!"

"Oh, lord," Elizabeth muttered, smiling to herself.

Their father chuckled at his own wit, then turned back to business. "Ella-belle, go and fetch Mrs. McKinley, tell her we've more guests. And Winthrop, as well. He will be most anxious to greet his brother." Ellen moved quickly, her eyes sliding to investigate the arrivals even as she left.

A young, dark, and handsome man grinned, brushing at snowflakes on his scarf. "Not so anxious, I trust. He'll be more pleased to see Davis than me."

"Surely not," Elinor's father scoffed warmly. "Indeed not." He turned, nearly tripping over his feet to check the following guests. "Come, come, my fine fellows. I will send my men out for the carriage once you're all settled. Don't fret, Mr. Morris, your fine horses are well in hand with Mr. Smythe."

Elinor's ears perked up and she stepped forward. "A carriage, Papa?"

Her father turned, his shoes skidding on the floor a touch. "Indeed, my pet. Got fretfully stuck in the mud on the southbound road from Buxton. Two broken axles and one wheel was quite done for. Nearly overturned, and the lot would have frozen there, completely stranded. Your uncle and I happened upon them on our way back in, and insisted they come with us."

"Lord Winthrop won't like to hear that," Elinor commented with a smile.

"No, love, it was not Mr. John's carriage," he corrected, patting the man in question on the back. "They arrived at the same time your uncle and I did with the weary travelers. A happy lot we make, eh?"

"Mr. Ames and Mr. Morris, do take yourselves on down to the kitchens," Uncle James was saying. "Sally will show you the way. Mrs. Larpenteur will warm you up creditably. Mr. Davis, do come along, and Mr. Rigby, of course."

Elinor looked at Elizabeth, and she returned her startled look, then both turned back to their father. "And they are all to stay, Papa?"

"But of course, they are!" he boomed. "It's Christmas! Gentlemen, do allow me to introduce two of my daughters. This is Elinor, and beside her, Elizabeth. My youngest you may have noticed hastening off for the housekeeper. Girls, Mr. John Winthrop, Mr. Davis, Mr. Rigby, Mr. Morris and Mr. Ames you see going down to the kitchens, they are the drivers, you know. Oh, and I do believe, Elinor, you might be acquainted with the last gentleman there."

Elinor hadn't seen another in the sudden crowd of them, and smiled politely mid-curtsey, "Oh?"

Her father nodded repeatedly, patting his waistcoat absently, still grinning. "Indeed. He's a London man, and was the poor fellow stranded in the mud." He turned towards the group, going up on his toes in an attempt to see. "Come, come, man, you will find only friends here."

A bit of shuffling, and then the man was before her.

Elinor stiffened, a gasp welling and dying in her throat.

"You do know Mr. Hugh Sterling, don't you, Elinor?"

Chapter Two

The unexpected is highly overrated.

-The Spinster Chronicles, 8 August 1818

It could have been worse, he supposed. She could have spat in his face or shrieked with horror or collapsed in a dead faint at his feet.

But anyone who had ever been on the receiving end of a disgusted glare from Elinor Asheley felt the impact of it in several suddenly aching places, and they burned most disconcertingly.

He was sure he'd experienced the sensation a time or two, but having spent the last few years at least mildly intoxicated at nearly every moment, he'd likely passed the experience off as indigestion from excessively rich food.

Still, the expression she'd worn at his presentation had left nobody in the room in any doubt of her feelings, except perhaps for her father, who, while all kindness and generosity himself, seemed the slightest bit oblivious.

They were all quickly shuffled off to vacant guest rooms to change and rest, if desired, while the servants of the house brought in all their things. While he appreciated having a moment of solitude after the morning he'd had, Hugh Sterling could honestly say he'd never been more uncomfortable in his entire life.

And that was saying a great deal indeed.

He wondered if his cousin Tony had arranged to have Elinor recommended to the army as a weapon yet. An enemy would certainly hesitate in the face of such a look, though it might not stop an offensive entirely. Still, the hesitation itself may be enough to turn the tide of a battle.

He hadn't meant to be here, and in fact, there was no place on earth he would rather be less than this. Of all the Spinsters, Elinor was the one who hated him the most.

They all had reason enough, but Elinor had seemed most violent about her hatred. The logical side of him wondered why, as she was one of the few he had not directly wounded in some way, but the more human side of him knew that would have very little to do with anything. Elinor Asheley was loyal to a fault, and it was quite an admirable thing.

Or it ought to be. At the moment, it was rather terrifying.

She would never believe what he had endured in the last several months. Would never believe the change that had occurred. She would never give him a moment to explain, apologize, cajole, or repent. He would ever be the villain in her eyes, the scum of the earth, if not the very devil, and it would make his waiting all the more unpleasant. He had barely managed to convince himself to take this sojourn as it was, and he feared the slightest provocation would send him back into hiding, setting back his recovery, as well.

He wasn't sure which would be worse.

It was the most maddening thing. He had never been particularly sensitive in his entire life, but suddenly, he was more skittish than any colt he'd ever seen, and twice as doubting.

A man on the road of repentance must adjust to all sorts of things.

He eyed himself in the long mirror on the other side of the room, wishing one's physical appearance changed when one's heart did. He was no longer a wastrel or rake, though he had never quite managed to fully attain the status of the latter, despite his association with them. The bitter thorn that had taken root within him had been torn out, and the damage had begun to heal. He no longer knew enmity or resentment, except for a select few who had sinned beyond all reconciliation.

He knew grief, he knew regret, and he knew self-loathing, all three in deep and profound ways. They had been his constant companions since the night his sister had nearly been ruined by the man he'd encouraged her to associate with. He had thought the man was his friend, and so had naively ignored every warning sign imaginable.

He had been forgiven by Alice, apparently, though he couldn't imagine how that was possible. Even his brother Francis had encouraged him to come home, that amends were not needed.

He hadn't listened to them. Couldn't bear to face them.

But now, he'd had enough of wallowing. He felt himself changed enough, thought that perhaps he might have been good enough to rejoin his family. For Christmas, at least.

And then the carriage had broken and become stuck, and he'd wondered at least a dozen times if this were not a sign that he was not, in fact, meant to go home to his family.

Instead, he was trapped. In the country. With her.

It seemed he had yet more fires to walk through before he would be deemed ready.

He already felt singed.

This was not good.

He smoothed down his straw-colored hair, which had grown too long in places, enough that his natural curl was noticeable, and he suddenly wished most fervently for a pair of shears. At least his clothing was more sensible than it once might have been. More tasteful in color and more reserved in style, the sort of look that would befit a gentleman.

Or at least avoid labeling him a dandy, as it once might have.

He had a reputation to expunge, and he would need all the help he could get.

If he could avoid being killed, mauled, maimed, or otherwise irreparably damaged by Elinor for however long he was here, he would have no problem with the rest of London.

Nobody hated him as much as Elinor.

He exhaled and met his own gaze squarely in the mirror. "Compliments of the season, Mr. Sterling," he muttered to himself.

Tugging on his coat, he moved from the room to venture into the rest of the house.

Deilingh was the epitome of everything a country house should be, with all the eccentricities one might expect from a country squire whose estate had been standing for a hundred years. Thick, darkly-stained wooden beams hung in the rafters, intricate carvings adorned the walls, and faded tapestries hung about, spots of wear beginning to show. The decor was comfortable and the arrangements well managed, despite the almost wild air of it all. It was clean, it was orderly, and seemed to extend in each direction as far as the eye could see.

He wondered faintly if the servants shared the dining room with the family all the time or if that was simply for the harvest celebrations. Not that it mattered, nor was it even his business. They could do as they liked here, and it was exactly that sort of thinking that could get him into trouble, well-intended or not.

Old habits were rather difficult to break, but he had spent the better part of seven months breaking all sorts of things once considered habit about himself.

How to prove such a change to anyone was equally as difficult.

How fortunate for him that he had the opportunity to begin the process with Elinor Asheley.

He was extremely tempted to cross himself for good measure as he proceeded down to the main part of the house.

As filled as the house had been with people when he'd arrived, and as bustling as it had seemed, now it was almost eerily silent, at least in the main entry. Not a single person, family, servant, or guest, could be seen. A house of this magnitude, and he was the lone individual in the vicinity?

Bizarre.

Perhaps Elinor had warned them all off, and they'd fled for their morality, abandoning him to an unfamiliar estate for Christmas alone.

He would not have put it past her.

A sudden burst of childish laughter suddenly reached his ears, and, intrigued, he headed towards the sound.

One of the drawing rooms had apparently been taken over by any and all festive greenery that could be had, and a pair of girls seemed more inclined to deck themselves in the greenery than do anything productive with it, and therein lay the source of the giggles.

He smiled as one of them began twirling while the other wrapped her in ribbon to accompany the evergreen bough draped across her, and he glanced around the rest of the room.

His breath froze in his chest, seizing up rather painfully.

The girls were not alone in the room. Also seated within were three grown women he didn't know, along with Mr. Partlowe, Mrs. Partlowe, and Elinor Asheley herself.

All of whom stared at him.

And he stared back.

Not knowing what else to do, he bowed a bit awkwardly. "Forgive my intrusion," he said, somehow managing to sound less awkward than he felt. "I heard the girls' laughter."

Mrs. Partlowe smiled with a degree of friendliness, while her sister seemed to grow even colder. Mr. Partlowe could not have cared less and returned his attention to the greenery before him.

"Have you settled in, Mr. Sterling?" Mrs. Partlowe asked in a carefully polite tone. "I know it can be a bit overwhelming coming into a full house like this, particularly when one is unfamiliar with it."

Hugh returned her smile, inclining his head in her direction. "I am, thank you. The home is lovely, and finely decorated. And as for it being full, I have yet to see that myself. I do know you have found yourself recently inundated with unexpected guests, for which I can only apologize for my part."

Elinor made a soft sound of disgruntlement, returning her attention to the greenery in her lap. A quick kick from her sister silenced the sound, though Mrs. Partlowe still looked completely innocent.

"Might I introduce my cousins and my aunt, Mr. Sterling?" Mrs. Partlowe offered, smiling as if to make up for her sister's disgust. She gestured towards the three women he did not know, all of whom had risen from the floor and waited for their presentation. "Mrs. Asheley, my aunt," she went on, as the youngest of the women curtseyed, confusing him to no end. "My cousin, Mrs. Layton." The taller woman with fair hair bobbed quickly, a dimple appearing in both cheeks. "My cousin, Mrs. Grover." The darkest woman managed to curtsey, though her obviously expanded girth made such things difficult.

"Anna, Hannah, Alice, this is Mr. Hugh Sterling, an acquaintance from London. His carriage was stranded in the poor road conditions, and he will be staying with us for Christmas."

Mrs. Grover chuckled, one hand going to her abdomen. "I pray you were not expecting tranquility, Mr. Sterling. Such a thing does not exist at Deilingh."

Hugh smiled at the good-humored woman and bowed. "I consider myself fortunate to find any place hospitable and welcoming for unexpected company, Mrs. Grover. I need no solitude in such circumstances."

"No, you are quite used to a rather riotous time of things, are you not?" Elinor muttered from her spot on the floor, separating branches of greenery carefully.

Someone hissed rather like a cat, and Hugh did his best to ignore it, wherever it had originated.

Mrs. Partlowe cleared her throat loudly. "Mrs. Asheley is my uncle's second wife, Mr. Sterling. I would not mention it except I saw your confusion when I referred to her as my aunt."

Had he been so careless as to reveal his surprise? Gads, he would never survive such a chaotic turn in this place if he did not have more reserve in his expression.

"I would never intend…" he began, apology ready on his lips.

"Tosh," Mrs. Asheley overrode, waving a hand. "I am quite used to it, I assure you. You need not bridle your tongue among this company. Two of my stepdaughters surpass me in age, and the girls you heard laughing are my daughter, Mariah, and my husband's granddaughter, Catherine. Can you greet Mr. Sterling, girls?"

The fair-haired girls gave identical curtseys, which wobbled, and immediately went back to their antics.

Hugh smiled at that. The children, it seemed, had the right way of things.

He returned his attention to the adults present. "It is a pleasure to meet you, ladies."

Mrs. Layton's dimples flashed again. "Glad you think so. You will find many, many more ladies to meet while you are here. Do not grow overwhelmed by the volume. None of us take offense readily, or we would all be offended every moment we are together."

"Some of us find offense thrust upon us," Elinor commented in a pleasant voice that would fool no one.

Hugh glanced over at her out of sheer reaction, knowing he should not.

Her glare at him was icier than the weather outside could ever be, and he was tempted to return to his waylaid carriage for safety.

He cleared his throat and, against all instincts towards self-preservation, stepped more fully into the room. "Might I be of some assistance in here?"

"Doubtful," Elinor replied without missing a beat.

This time Elinor received a kick that was not so discreet.

"What my sister means," Mrs. Partlowe said quite firmly, "is that we are all rather hopeless, and it would be monstrously unkind to drag you into this melee. But do please be seated, if you think our conversation might interest you."

There was no way in the world to know if it would, but considering the only people he really knew in this house were the ones in this room, he might as well stay. One of those people would love to see him drawn and quartered, it was true, but knowing that at least prevented his being surprised by such an attack.

And surely there were enough sensible family members present to restrain her.

He couldn't say anything resembling such about the others at Deilingh, as he wasn't acquainted with them as yet.

What if there were more Elinors within?

A shudder rippled through him, and he opted to sit on a nearby ottoman for safety, all the actual seating of the room being currently occupied with various items of greenery.

"Is it not a bit early to hang the holiday greenery?" he queried of the room in general. "Christmas Eve is nearly a week away."

He saw Elinor stiffen, and he wondered, faintly, if everything he said would irritate her, and if it did, if he could manage to rate the level of irritation based on what he said. Not that he would return to his former villainous ways, but if, in being a respectable houseguest, he could still manage to sin against her sensibilities.

Without actually sinning at all.

"It is indeed," Mrs. Asheley replied from her pile of evergreen boughs. "And while we do tend towards bending the traditional ways in some things, in this we are mostly traditional. We merely organize and prepare greenery for now, and it will go up the evening before Christmas Eve." She shrugged, smiling. "It gives us an occupation that keeps us out of mischief, I suppose."

Mrs. Layton laughed and gave her stepmother a wry look. "Who in here do you suspect of getting into mischief?"

Mrs. Grover winced and indicated her abdomen. "This one, for one. The child thinks it's already Christmas Day and is dancing on my ribs."

The married women all grimaced sympathetically, while Mr. Partlowe looked mildly uncomfortable by the conversation.

Elinor frowned in confusion, then looked at Hugh, probably against her will, and the frown deepened markedly.

What had he done? He was simply sitting as he had been invited to, and she looked as though he had threatened a puppy.

Hugh returned his attention to the more pleasant members of the family, smiling with as much kindness as he could. "My mother would be beside herself. She fully holds to the tradition that no greenery could even be in our house before Christmas Eve. She was convinced it would bring us bad luck in the coming year."

"More than she already had?" came Elinor's low reply, though it seemed he was the only one to catch it.

The other ladies laughed instead. "And where do your opinions on the subject lie, Mr. Sterling?" Mrs. Asheley asked as she began to fold some boughs into each other.

Hugh shrugged a shoulder. "I am rather of the opinion that a person makes their own luck, ma'am. For good or for ill, we hold the power in ourselves to determine our fate."

"That's a distressing thought for some," Elinor said without reserve, her tone sounding mild for the first time. "What if a person has led a disastrous life and their fate is to match it? Hardly encouraging, wouldn't you agree?"

The pointed nature of her look left no doubt as to whom she was referring, not that Hugh had questioned it one way or the other. He met her gaze as squarely as he could, tipping his chin down enough to be quite direct.

"Do you believe in redemption, Miss Asheley? Or that a person can change when brought to an awareness of past mistakes? Or are we doomed to live as we have lived, even if we no longer wish to?"

Her eyes widened and she sat back on her heels, staring at him in outright bewilderment.

"That sounds like a question for our uncle, Mr. Perry," Mrs. Layton said with a hint of a laugh. "He is very much concerned with all things spiritual, particularly with regards to one's soul. He would never abide by the more pagan idea of fate or luck."

"No, indeed," Mrs. Grover agreed, nodding firmly. "But Mr. Sterling does ask a rather good question, I think. What is Christmas for but hope and the chance to improve one's self?"

Hugh heard them, acknowledged their answers, but kept his attention fixed on Elinor. It was her answer he was most curious to hear, if she would take it in the proper spirit. He had backed her into a corner, he knew, and he was quite pleased to have done it. What would she do now, before her family, when the target of all her hatred had questioned her so?

Her wide, blue eyes blinked, the smallest of furrows appearing between her trim brows. He watched as her throat worked, and noted, for the first time, what a slender, pale, elegant throat it was. She wore a small gold cross there, and the cross itself sat tucked rather neatly right in the notch at the base. Why that should attract his attention, he couldn't say, but attracted he was, and it took all his power not to lower his eyes to that maddening cross to examine it further.

Much safer to stay with her eyes, swirling with confusion, distaste, and a hint of, dare he say it, interest. Fascinated by him, was she? Well, if she stopped attempting to have him beheaded at every waking moment, she might truly have something to be interested in.

And those eyes the color of a fair sky in winter might look a little less cold and a little less indignant.

Merciful heavens, was he finding attractive features in Elinor Asheley? He might have to speak to that Perry uncle of theirs, if the man was in holy orders. Clearly, Hugh Sterling had been overpowered by a demon.

No, that wasn't fair. Elinor Asheley was an attractive woman, as any man with eyes would attest. It was only the snarling manner of her nature that kept anyone from feeling the need to do so.

Or the ability to.

"Well, Miss Asheley?" he pressed, not entirely sure why he was doing so. He only knew that her answer mattered in some way.

Somehow.

Elinor wet her lips carefully, then straightened. "A person can change, certainly, and redemption is possible. For some."

He almost smiled at her caveat, but somehow, he managed to avoid it.

"The only question I have," she continued, her eyes flashing with an intriguing light as they stayed on his, "is the quality and sincerity of that change. What is to prevent a person from changing yet again? Perhaps into something far worse." She quirked a daring brow, her lips forming an impetuous line.

Oh, she was clever, and this time he had to smile, just a little. "Or into something far better."

The furrow between her brows deepened into an outright scowl, despite the fact that all of the other women in the room were nodding in agreement with him. Or perhaps *because* they were nodding in agreement.

Hugh raised a brow back at her, echoing hers to him.

He watched the fiery woman inhale, then exhale with would-be calm before pasting a bland smile on her face.

"Mr. Partlowe," she said suddenly, "you're an educated man."

Her brother-in-law seemed surprised to be addressed and looked up from his focused work on the boughs in his lap.

"I like to think so," he carefully replied.

Elinor raised the bunch of mistletoe in her lap, tilting her head in question. "When did the hanging of mistletoe begin?"

Mr. Partlowe thought for a moment. "Well," he eventually began, "the practice of gathering mistletoe at all in England started in the second century by ancient druids, as far as we know. At the beginning of winter, they gathered the plant from what they considered to be the sacred oak. It was seen as a symbol in that culture, one of harmony, hope, and peace."

The others in the room were listening now, and, sensing he had a moderately captive audience, the young giggling girls aside, he warmed to the subject. "Sprigs of mistletoe were hung in various homes in the hopes of heralding good fortune in the coming year. Did you know that mistletoe could also be used for medicinal purposes?"

"I did not," Elinor commented in all sincerity, shaking her head.

"It's true," Mr. Partlowe insisted. "The plants were also used for medicinal purposes. It was believed they could promote female fertility and be an antidote for poison."

Elinor nodded now, her eyes wide. "Fascinating, Mr. Partlowe. And…"

"But," Mr. Partlowe went on, ignoring her attempts to end his explanation, "in Norse mythology, the mistletoe was a sign of friendship and love. It's widely believed that it is this tradition that has led to the current customs regarding mistletoe."

Hugh bit back a laugh as Elinor stared at her brother-in-law, the cursed plant still in her grasp.

"Indeed, what a thought," she replied, her tone tight. Then she cleared her throat. "And is it bad luck if the mistletoe falls?"

Mr. Partlowe reared back a little, his thick brows rising. "I couldn't say for certain, the details of such are unclear."

"Would you think it would be a bad thing?" Elinor pressed, returning her attention to Hugh, keeping her tone ambivalent, even if her gaze was murderous. "Perhaps unlucky?"

What in the world was she getting at? Why would he be blamed for mistletoe falling anywhere? Was she plotting to curse him with falling mistletoe in the hopes that he would flee the house and her life forever in dismay? She would be disappointed, if that were the case.

Mr. Partlowe had no such suspicions. "That seems reasonable, yes," he mused. "Most likely ill-fated love, if you believe in such customs."

Elinor smiled, if one could consider such an evil curve to an otherwise impeccable set of lips a smile. "And what if one should have mistletoe thrown at them?"

Ah, there it was.

Now Mr. Partlowe looked alarmed. "Well, I can hardly see how that would be a good thing either, particularly with the customs being what they are…"

Hugh continued to stare at Elinor without shame, daring her to follow through with the unspoken threat after building it up to such an extent.

She tilted her chin ever so slightly, and he thought, for the space of several heartbeats, that she might actually do it.

Then the moment passed, and she shrugged, dropping her gaze back to the white berries and greenery in her lap. "Let us hope that no mistletoe should fall, then."

"Or be thrown," Hugh murmured, not bothering to also avert his gaze.

Elinor Asheley was a fascinating creature, and it surprised him to admit it. Her golden hair was plaited in a crown of sorts, though a few ringlets hung in front of her ears and a few curled tendrils flowed from the base of the crown itself. The effect gave her an almost angelic appearance, which was quite disconcerting.

Almost, because she had yet to smile as he imagined an angel would. Disconcerting, because Elinor Asheley was no angel. Fascinating, but not angelic.

Her eyes flicked up to his and widened when she caught him staring.

Was he still staring? He must have been, but why?

Just… why?

Elinor scowled with more darkness than she had yet, but her cheeks flushed pink with such haste that it seemed to startle her. She huffed and got to her feet, storming out of the room, notably taking the mistletoe with her.

Hugh smiled as she left, wondering about that blush he'd seen.

Perhaps that was why he stared.

Not likely, but perhaps.

Chapter Three

Assumptions may get a body into trouble. One must never ever assume anything, unless one would have assumptions made about themselves. Or is that judgment? This author is not entirely clear, though surely, they are interchangeable in this case.

-The Spinster Chronicles, 16 September 1817

This was going to be the worst Christmas ever. Elinor was absolutely certain of it.

She had no idea what Hugh Sterling was about, but his attempts at polite conversation had irritated her beyond belief. She was destined to bruise from her sister's repeated kicks, but it was worth it to risk running her mouth as she wished. Hugh Sterling would not dare to insult her in her own home, so she would take every advantage offered.

The trouble was that he was not reacting as much as she would wish, given the beautiful timing of her barbs.

He just seemed to sit there and be amused by it all.

Amusing, was it, for his character to be so maligned by someone who knew exactly what he was capable of? It would only show his true nature, if he were to continue in such a way. He was a master in the art of villainy and depravity, and she had no qualms at all about letting her entire family know it.

The only trouble she could possibly imagine would come from the quarters of her parents or Uncle James. They all held great stock in being hospitable and warm, and during the holiday season, it was even more pronounced. They were the merriest of people, and they would never hear of behaving with anything less.

She would never have gotten away with her antics in the blue room had one of them been present.

Strategy would be key to preventing her family from being drawn in by Hugh if she wanted to avoid being resoundingly scolded publicly.

She would never live that shame down, particularly if he were to witness it.

Her abrupt departure from the blue room couldn't be helped, particularly with the creature staring at her so. It was unnerving in the extreme, and she wished, most heartily, that one of the other Spinsters were in the house to commiserate with her on the subject. No one else would understand the full scope of this atrocity and the potential for future evils he presented.

Even now, she was huffing as she strode down to the kitchens, determined to speak to the drivers that had been so unfortunate as to also be stranded at Deilingh. They would be able to answer a few of her more important questions, and she was in desperate need of answers.

The kitchens were bustling, as they always seemed to be at this time of year, and Mrs. Larpenteur was right in the thick of it, ordering everyone about with an efficiency that would have made Wellington proud. Elinor glanced around the overheated space and moved to the table where two weary men sat.

"Excuse me, gentlemen," she said politely as she approached. "Would you happen to be the coachmen that came in with my father not long ago?"

They both rose quickly and bowed.

"Yes, miss," the taller one said, his voice almost shockingly deep.

"Please thank your father for allowing us to stay," the stouter man said, his bristled mustache twitching slightly. "Most generous."

Elinor smiled rather ruefully. "I can answer for my father, sir, in saying it's no trouble, and that it is entirely my father's nature to do so. I wonder if you both might answer a question for me."

The drivers looked at each other, then back at her.

"If we are able, miss," the burly one said.

She nodded at that. "The unfortunate damage to the carriage that was stuck. How long do you expect the repairs will take? I would hate for your master to miss celebrating Christmas as he had planned, if it can be avoided."

The tall man smiled with more warmth than her lie deserved. "Generally, it depends on the skill of the craftsmen to be found and how quickly they can accommodate our needs. But your uncle has seen to it that repairs are already underway, so it is possible that the carriage could be ready in a day or two."

"Marvelous!" Elinor exclaimed, clapping her hands. "Mr. Sterling will be so pleased!"

"But," the other interjected, "we must also consider the weather, miss. The roads may not be passable. Our coach carrying Mr. John Winthrop struggled, as well, and we were coming from the south."

Elinor continued to nod. "Of course, of course. But if the roads improve, he might arrive in time to celebrate Christmas with his family!"

The tall driver bowed in acknowledgement. "Indeed, miss. He just might."

She thanked them for their indulgence and fairly skipped out of the kitchens, delighted by the news.

If the carriage could be mended as quickly as they suggested, Hugh would be out of their house in two days at the most. She would clear the roads herself with her bare hands if she had to, or bring wooden slats to cover the muddy ruts, or pull the blasted coach herself if it would see him far away from her.

She could save Christmas for herself and her family, if this all went smoothly.

Hugh Sterling would not ruin this for her.

Elinor sighed as she reached the main level again, then looked at the greenery in her hands, which she had somehow forgotten in all the fuss.

Ugh. Mistletoe. Cursed plant with its cursed tradition encouraging the kissing of unwed girls by men with nothing honorable to occupy their time or their minds.

There was nothing wrong with the married couples who chose

to continue the traditions, if they so desired, but really, what good could such a plant do for those without such ties?

It would be only too tempting an opportunity for a blackguard the likes of Hugh Sterling to take advantage of.

Her chest seized as she considered her innocent, naive younger sisters. They had yet to fully engage in a London Season, and they would know nothing of his machinations, or indeed the nature of any man with similar inklings.

She had to protect them. To save them. The Spinsters were not here to help her; she was on her own. It was time, then, to take matters into her own hands.

She set the mistletoe down behind a tapestry before striding towards the large parlor at the back of the house where the family was more inclined to gather, if they gathered at all.

It was rare that they did.

As she approached the room, she knew that this was one of those rare times. She could see four cousin husbands as well as Uncle Dough standing behind one of the sofas, which would indicate that they were unable to sit upon it. Aunt Beatrice and Aunt Julia sat in their usual chairs against the wall, glasses of port in hand.

How very typical.

The only question was whether the entire family was within, or only a portion of them, and if their guests had joined them.

She strode into the room, smiling for all, turning her attention to the front of the room, as the others did, where her father was talking.

The smile faded at once when she saw Hugh standing near him, smiling sheepishly.

Hugh Sterling did not know how to be sheepish.

She frowned at once as she stood next to Uncle Dough. "What's happening?" she whispered.

Uncle Dough grunted, his girth shifting with an inhale. "Your father feels the need to make a speech about your Mr. Sterling there."

"He is not *my* Mr. Sterling, Uncle Dough," Elinor muttered snappishly. "Far from it. And what about him?"

Uncle Dough indicated Hugh with a flick of his plump hand. "He's been convinced to stay through Christmas, at your father and uncle's insistence."

Elinor stared at Uncle Dough in horror. "He's what? But I've just spoken to the drivers, and they told me that the wheel and axle could be fixed in a day or two. Why remain the further few days?"

"Because, as your father so eloquently said, 'it would be deuced uncharitable to send a man off the moment his coach is better with Christmas so near.'" Uncle Dough scoffed, not nearly as filled with Christian generosity as the others. "Doesn't say much of Sterling's festive plans that he is so free to give them up to remain with us, does it?"

The sound that escaped Elinor was not entirely ladylike, but it bore no profanities.

Discernable ones, anyway.

"I doubt Mr. Sterling is above accepting what is freely offered," Elinor informed Uncle Dough, "and I further doubt he had anything better to do with his time. A man of his nature and proclivity never does. Why not remain with a moderately wealthy, generous family, and take advantage of the situation? It may have been that he sabotaged his own coach for the sake of a more comfortable situation."

Uncle Dough gave her a sidelong look as her father continued to speak to the rest of the family. "You take quite a critical view of the man."

Elinor folded her arms, shaking her head firmly. "I only speak as I find, Uncle Dough. He is nothing but trouble, and the worst of it at that. I am all too well acquainted with him in London."

"Should we warn your father, then?"

If only she could.

She shook her head once more, dipping her chin to glare at the intruder darkly. "It won't make any difference, and you know it. Papa is determined to be kind-hearted to a fault, and this, I can assure you, is a fault. A rather vile one."

Uncle Dough grunted, returning his attention to the front of the room, tilting his head a touch. "I appreciate your view on the matter, dear, to be sure, but… He doesn't seem particularly vile. A bit gaunt in the face, perhaps. Peaky, to be sure, and not quite tall enough to be imposing, as one might wish to be. Still, he complimented your mother creditably, showed no disdain with the children, and I have yet to see him scowl."

"Even reptiles can smile when they have to," Elinor insisted, refusing to clap when the others did at something or other her father said.

"Don't snarl," her uncle advised in a low tone, betraying her slightly by offering a few claps of his hands. "It will make your displeasure more evident, and someone will comment."

Elinor sputtered softly. "Whatever would that be like?"

"Elinor…" He raised a scolding brow. "Don't ruin Christmas for the family in an attempt to rid the house of Mr. Sterling."

"Oh, I don't intend to, Uncle Dough," she assured him, allowing her lips to curve just a little. "But I do very much intend to inform our Mr. Sterling of the expectations for his stay with us. And the limitations."

"*Our* Mr. Sterling? Interesting," Uncle Dough grunted and sipped some suspicious-looking punch. "Suit yourself." He moved away from her, ambling towards some of her cousins, one or two of whom seemed markedly interested in their now not-as-temporary guest.

"Don't even think about it, girls," she told them, though they hadn't a hope of hearing her, muttering the words under her breath as she was.

Hugh Sterling wasn't going to ruin their Christmas, and he most certainly wasn't going to ruin hers.

But if she could find a way to ruin his without ruining anyone else's along the way, she would find it to be quite a festive gift indeed.

Amazingly, there wasn't a single opportunity to say anything to Hugh until they had finished supper and all the family and guests included were moving towards the drawing room for some light evening entertainment, if not dancing.

The one time in her life when she actually sought opportunity to speak with the vile man, and she couldn't even manage it.

Though, in all honesty, she couldn't be blamed for it.

Somehow, Hugh Sterling had made himself so widely agreeable

among her family that he was in company almost constantly. If it wasn't her uncle or father, it was the cousin husbands wanting tales of London, as they rarely ventured there, or it was her unmarried female cousins trying to engender a good impression on an eligible visitor.

And then there were the children.

Elinor could not understand it, but the children seemed to flock to him, and he never once swatted them away or seemed remotely displeased. Any man in his situation would have every reason to be markedly annoyed with the rambunctious children of his hosts, particularly when he would have little enough experience with children at all.

Hugh Sterling seemed as pleased to see them as he was to see any given person.

It wasn't possible. The man she knew was not pleased by anything but sin, idleness, and villainy. He sought to make himself a nuisance just for amusement and took great delight in voicing displeasure. He was evil, he was spoiled, and he was smug.

He was also changed.

In looks, at least. His hair was a shade darker, his stature less proper, his jaw more angular. He had lost the pasty, bland look he had always worn before, and the youthful tint to his features. His eyes were clearer than she could ever remember seeing, and without the bloodshot background, the blue in them seemed to stand out more brightly.

He was an older Hugh Sterling, and somehow not just with the loss of some weight, as had clearly occurred.

If she did not know better, she would also have noted a newfound level of maturity in him.

Considering he had only ever been as mature as an ill-mannered twelve-year-old, that was no special accomplishment.

And she refused to accept that a more attractive Hugh Sterling was a more mature one.

Or a truly changed one.

Or anything worthy of praise or positive attention.

Until she could swear before God otherwise, he would still be her nemesis.

And while she could, she would take the opportunity to let him know that.

"Mr. Sterling," she called softly as she approached him, carefully smiling for all appearances. "A moment?"

He turned and gave her a look, which she pointedly ignored. "Miss Asheley. Of course, I am at your service."

His tone was not nearly as polite as his words were, and her smile became pointedly strained, the ribbon at her throat feeling like a noose.

"Lovely," she ground out, barely managing to not snarl.

"Is that how you would like me to compliment you?" he inquired, clasping his hands behind his back with a slight bow. "Very well, Miss Asheley, in that shade of red, I find you…"

"Shut up," she hissed, gathering her skirts in her hands and huffing away from him with a jerk of her head. "That's not funny."

When her steps softened in their tread, he said, "It was not an attempt at humor. I take paying compliments quite seriously."

Elinor scowled at him as she paused at a grand window not far from the drawing room door, but far enough away to avoid being overheard. "I would, too, if I were so out of practice giving sincere compliments."

Hugh's mouth twitched into a hint of a smile. "Forgive me, I thought you were, particularly with the male sex."

"Show me a man worth complimenting, and I will do so."

Now he did smile, though he kept it restrained. "Shall I fetch your father? Your uncle? Your brother or cousins or Mr. John Winthrop, perhaps?"

Elinor rolled her eyes and knitted her fingers, shaking her head. "Unbelievable. You're an impossible sot even without the influence of drink."

"I believe that is called being a Sterling, Miss Asheley," he informed her, giving a sage nod. "See also my brother Lord Sterling, and our cousin Tony. I believe you know him well."

This was going nowhere at a breakneck pace.

"Allow me to be quite direct, Mr. Sterling," she all but barked, her eyes flicking towards the open drawing room door.

"It is your home, Miss Asheley, I will allow you almost anything."

Elinor paused, clenching her teeth so hard her jaw ached. "You will not ruin Christmas for my family," she told him.

He lifted one brow. "I have no intention of doing so. It would be quite rude."

She ignored that. "You will not speak with my sisters unaccompanied."

Hugh nodded. "That is generally the polite way of things."

In lieu of screeching, she dug her nails into the palms of her hands. "And if I catch you with any of my relations in an empty corridor, Hugh Sterling, so help me…"

His expression turned into one of complete disbelief. "I didn't get stranded here deliberately, you know. I had a set destination, and it was not your family's country home at Christmas."

"I wouldn't trust you to not take advantage of whatever situation you found yourself in with the express purpose of furthering your own selfish interests," she snapped, positively fuming now.

The corridor was almost completely silent, only the echoes of conversation in the drawing room audible as Hugh stared at her, his eyes searching.

"Out of curiosity, how many counts of villainy do you think me guilty of? I'm wondering if I've reached the level of 'demon of hell' yet."

Somehow, she found his statement amusing, and the urge to laugh welled up, though she tamped it down quite forcefully.

"It's difficult to say," she managed to express with surprising calmness. "You blessed us all by staying away from London for so many months, I hardly know how many sins you engaged in while thus occupied."

Hugh's face suddenly contorted into one of sheer torment, and he took a step towards her. "Do not dare to presume that I exiled myself only to sink further into the life of misery I had gotten myself into," he hissed, his words sounding as though they rasped painfully against his throat. "You have no idea what I have suffered. What I have endured. No matter how you hate me, Elinor Asheley, it cannot compare to how I have hated myself of late."

She had not expected that outburst, not in the slightest. She had hoped he had felt some remorse for what had happened to Alice, but this was beyond anything.

She stared at him in shock, gaping. Then she swallowed. "Hate is a strong word," she reminded him.

"The emotions behind it are stronger," he insisted, seeming to recover some part of himself and turning away. He moved to the window, his face taking on new shadows and angles in the moonlight, and none of them softening him. "I am not the man I was, though I know full well that it may never be believed as possible. That is my burden to bear." He lowered his head, then glanced towards her. "I pray you find some way to avoid making it a heavier one than it already is."

Elinor tilted her head, unwittingly curious. "Are you asking for my forgiveness?"

Hugh turned towards her again but did not approach. "I do not expect you to forgive the man I was," he told her, his voice dark and low. "I only ask that you see me for the man that I am now."

Elinor frowned at his answer, not in displeasure, but in confusion.

It was a bit of an odd request, but not an unreasonable one. In fact, it might have been the simplest request she had ever heard. Was that not what they all wanted in life? To be seen for who they were without prejudice or judgment?

Would she not want to be seen that way?

She pursed her lips, a question forming and dying at the same moment. What could she ask? How could she respond?

How could anyone?

Hugh watched her for a moment, then exhaled faintly, straightening. "I know you might not believe this, Elinor, but I mean you no harm. I mean your family no harm. I mean to redeem myself in the eyes of the world, and if I have to start with yours, so be it. Consider what I've asked, if you will. See if you can manage that much kindness for a man like me."

He bowed surprisingly deeply, then moved to the drawing room without another word.

Elinor watched him go, utterly bewildered now.

An emotion was welling, surging within her, and it turned her cheeks hot and made her eyes burn. She felt almost twitchy, her fingers tightening against each other in strained convulsions.

Shame. It was shame that burned down her neck and along her ears. It was shame that made her stomach clench and her knees tremble. Shame that brought tears to her eyes and shook her lungs on each breath.

Shame? How could she feel shame with regards to Hugh Sterling?

She pressed her hand to her quaking heart. She didn't understand it, but she dared not deny it.

It was shame that she felt, and the need to repent of… something.

She swallowed hard. See him for the man he was, he asked.

Well, she wasn't sure that was possible, but she could try.

For some bizarre reason, at this moment, she actually wanted to.

She also wanted to throw mistletoe at his head for turning her emotions on her, but there was no mistletoe at hand.

More's the pity.

Elinor cleared her suddenly clogged throat and brushed at her skirts, then did her best to sweep into the drawing room without any signs of strain.

Hugh was already deep in conversation with Lawrence, one of the more tolerable cousin husbands, apparently none the worse for wear after his outburst.

Acting now or acting then? Or accustomed to quickly recovering? There was no telling with him, and she wasn't sure why it mattered.

But it did.

"Ah, my dear girl, so delighted to have you here at last," her father blustered as he came over, his cheeks rosy, possibly from too much port.

"Papa?" Elinor tried to smile as he took her hands exuberantly. "I did not realize I had kept you waiting."

Her father shook his head with just as much bluster. "Not at all, love, not at all. We only needed you to complete the quartet."

"Quartet?" she repeated. She looked across the room in confusion, then saw her sisters standing by the pianoforte, looking back at her.

Oh. *That* quartet.

She'd completely forgotten about that little tradition.

She blanched at the thought. "Papa, we have not rehearsed at all. And normally, we don't perform until…"

"Yes, yes, my dear, but we have guests this year, and we must allow for adjustments." He patted her hand and smiled with all the fatherly fondness he possessed. "Just sing a song you already know, and we'll excuse any lack of harmonies."

Oh, was that all? None of them were particularly gifted singers, but they were accomplished enough, and when joined together, sounded better than any of them alone.

They were used to performing for family.

They never performed for guests.

Grumbling under her breath, Elinor moved towards her sisters, feeling the eyes of the room on her.

"Sorry!" Emma whispered when she reached them. "We didn't have a choice!"

Elinor shook her head. "What are we singing?"

"*Adeste Fideles*?" Elizabeth suggested, looking just as panicked, though she was far and away the best singer of the sisters. "We did all right when we sang that one."

"I didn't," Ellen pointed out sourly.

The sisters glared at her. "You were ill that year," Elinor reminded her. "You remember your part?"

Her youngest sister nodded, still looking sullen.

"Fine. Let's get this over with." Elinor sighed and turned to face the room, all of whom had gathered around to hear them.

Without a sign from any of the sisters, Emma sat behind the pianoforte and began to play their introduction, the soft, lower strains beginning to fill the room.

Elizabeth began first, her clear voice ringing out with the warm, husky tones the song required.

Elinor joined her in harmony, keeping her eyes constantly scanning across those in the room, forcing her expression to remain as delighted as possible.

Emma and Ellen came in together, adding yet another dimension to the harmonies of the song, and the four of them began to find themselves moving in near-perfect synchronization with each other's notes. Their voices were all so similar in timbre and sound that the combination of them tended to lend them a more polished air than it was in reality.

As the song commenced, the faces of their audience transitioned to individual smiles all around, and without exception. Their mother had tears, and their father seemed fit to bursting with pride, but those were reactions they were well versed in.

The guests experiencing this Asheley sister phenomenon bore similar expressions of pleased bewilderment, which was to be expected, under these circumstances.

But one face, in particular, held Elinor's attention, much against her will.

Hugh Sterling bore the awestruck look of a man seeing an angel or goddess, though how he managed to smile while so completely agape was miraculous.

That wasn't what captivated her.

It was his complete fixation on her. He did not look at any of her sisters as they sang.

Just her.

There was no way he could have made out her voice above the rest, they had it on good assurance that such a thing was impossible.

But he could.

She had no idea how she knew that just from his expression, but know it she did.

It was the most terrifying, vulnerable realization she had ever felt. She was not a gifted singer, it was well known, and only in a chorus with her sisters was she even remotely capable. She would never be a soloist, and she did not wish to be.

Yet for him, in this moment, she might as well have been. He ought to have heard Elizabeth's voice, or even Emma's, if he were to hear anything worth hearing.

But no, it was clear that he was hearing her.

And there was no sign of mockery, superiority, or disgust in him. It was the most genuine she had ever seen him appear.

While he looked at her.

Her.

Something in her heart began to race, and she wrenched her gaze away, focusing on the beaming Uncle Dough as they neared the end of the song.

The piano began to fade, and their voices faded with it, trailing off into a warm finish that seemed to hang in the air for a moment.

Then the room applauded, and Elinor found her gaze returning, somehow, to that of Hugh Sterling.

He still looked at her alone. He still smiled.

And he applauded them, or her, as his smile grew.

At which time, that traitorous heart of hers skipped and raced as though they had sung a jig.

Chapter Four

In winter, we find ourselves confined in places and involved in activities we might never engage in were the weather conditions more appropriate. One should never judge a person by their winter habits.

-The Spinster Chronicles, 4 February 1818

Hugh sat quietly in the library, enjoying the moment's reprieve from the complete chaos of Deilingh. A book lay open in his lap, though he only pretended to scan the pages before him.

He had never been a very great reader, but there were hardly better options for how to spend his time this morning. He had certainly inquired, but this, it seemed, would be his position for some time.

Difficult to believe as it might have been for some.

A small hint of a smile lit one corner of his mouth briefly as a particular sound met his ears. He forced his expression into blankness and focused on the pretend reading of his book.

There was a faint shuffling, a restrained giggle, two sniffles, rustling, and then…

"RAH!" came the shout of multiple little voices, while two sets of little hands landed on his shoulders.

He gasped dramatically and tossed his now closed book in the air. "Heavens above!"

More giggles rent the air, and Hugh sank down into the chair as though their hands pressed him into it. "Oh no! Oh, I can't escape!

Oh no!"

"We got him!" one of the young boys cried, whooping as he dashed around the chair. "He's melting!"

Hugh reacted accordingly, continuing to slide down his chair with agonized moans before flopping to the ground and rolling about until he lay still, face down on the rug.

He remained as still as possible, barely breathing.

One by one, he heard their footsteps approach him, and then, with great hesitation, a few bold fingers began to poke at his back and shoulders. Then, the hesitation seemed to fade and the fingers became more insistent, jabbing between his shoulder blades and into the back of his head.

"Did we really kill him?" one of the girls asked, sounding less timid and more dubious in her question. "Just by giving him a fright?"

"Tommy, check if he's dead," another girl asked.

Hugh waited where he lay, and, sure enough, a moment later his eyelid was pried open.

He roared to life, making the children screech in fright and dismay as he rose to his knees and began to bark like a dog.

It turned out that his attackers consisted of four boys and five girls, none older than eight years of age, and the youngest perhaps only three. They bore enough similarity in features to all be related, without question, but also bore enough differences to argue the degree of said relationship.

"Run!" one of the girls cried as Hugh continued to bark.

They all did, without question, but rather than charge for the door, they moved further into the library.

Hugh grinned, and gave chase, barking madly, wheezing laughs in between each bark.

The screeches of the children turned to mad giggles, and when one of the girls had the ingenious idea to try petting the rabid dog, Hugh immediately rolled to his back and began panting and kicking his left leg, just as his father's dog always did when petted.

Tickling the dog then became the game and seeing which of them could make him howl in the silliest manner.

It turned out that Hugh actually possessed the ability to howl in a desperately silly manner, and with some variety.

He'd never figured that out before. He really couldn't remember barking on hands and knees or rolling about on the floor panting, so perhaps that followed.

Following silly howling, they hunted for grouse, which the canine Hugh was most adept at fetching accordingly, though he really was quite miserable at getting the grouse out of their hiding places in order to be shot.

At least according to the hunters, he was. He thought he had performed the task admirably, but he was, it seemed, quite mistaken.

Ah, well, he had never been a sportsman.

"I want to play in the snow!" one of the girls suddenly whined, sinking to the ground with a dramatic flick of her skirts.

Phoebe, if he recollected correctly, was the youngest of the party, and seemed to bore easily. He sat up and gave her a kind, pitying smile.

"A bit bored with the silly dog, Phoebe?"

The girl nodded, jutting her lower lip out in an impressive pout. "It snowed more last night. I want to play in the snow!"

One of her cousins sighed and plopped down beside her on the floor. "Pheebs, it's too cold. The mamas said we'll freeze, so we must stay inside. We aren't even going to go for a sleigh ride today. Uncle Dough says maybe tomorrow."

"Uncle Dough?" Hugh repeated, leaning on one elbow. "Which one is that?"

The tallest boy leaned against a bookcase with a sigh. "He's nearly as round as he is tall."

"He is not!" one of the girls snickered, snorting softly into a chubby hand.

"Fairly," came a response from the only boy whose name Hugh could remember.

"Well, I know who he means, at any rate, Tommy," Hugh said with a laugh. "So, whose father is Uncle Dough, hmm?"

All of the children looked at him as though he had sprouted three additional heads. "No one," the majority said at once.

Even little Phoebe laughed. "Uncle Dough isn't a papa!"

Of course not. Silly Hugh, what an idea.

He shook his head, laughing even as the children continue to giggle at his apparent idiocy. This family, he would easily admit, was peculiar.

Warm and generous, but peculiar.

"What if Mr. Sterling takes us outside?" Little Phoebe asked, brightening pointedly, her white-blond curls bouncing in the light of the room.

Hugh raised a brow. "I'm not brave enough to stand up to all the mothers in the house, poppet." He looked over both shoulders pointedly, then back at her before whispering, "There's a fair few of them, you know."

"And they tend to forget which ones they belong to," Tommy said with a grunt that was older than his years. "Only yesterday, Aunt Millie scolded me and told Nanny not to give me dessert."

"Tsk tsk." Hugh shook his head in sympathy. "And where is Nanny now?"

All of the children shrugged, their shoulders bobbing up and down in a poorly choreographed dance of sorts.

Hugh sighed, making a face as he thought. "Well, we cannot just sit here in the library forever. So, our options are to go and find Nanny…"

"No!" the boys and the oldest of the girls cried.

"Or," Hugh continued with a nod of agreement, "we devise winter games that will not subject us to the dreaded freeze the mamas warned you about."

That got their attention.

The children stared at him, curious and eager, and the girls, at least, sat up, giving him their full attention.

"How, Mr. Sterling?" another of the blond girls asked, folding her arms rather like he'd seen Elinor do a time or two.

"Well…" He frowned and hummed at her. "What was your name again?"

She scowled, again like her elder relation. "Amelia. A gentleman wouldn't forget."

Hugh smirked at her sharp response. She was the spit of Elinor, and where that once would have disgusted him, it now amused him.

As Elinor now amused him.

And fascinated him.

"As we were not properly, nor officially introduced, Miss Amelia," Hugh replied with a warm smile, "I believe I may be excused while still maintaining my gentleman status."

She looked doubtful, but she offered no argument against it.

He looked around at the children, speculating without giving anything away. "Let me see… Hmm… I can't decide…"

"On what?" one of the older boys demanded.

Hugh shook his head, heaving a dramatic sigh. "On who would make the best snowman."

The children exchanged bewildered looks before returning their attention to him, most bearing the appearance of questioning his sanity.

"A snowman?" Amelia repeated. "One of us?"

"I do *not* want to be covered in snow!" Phoebe insisted firmly, folding her arms with a sharp hrmph of disgruntlement.

Hugh grinned swiftly, shaking his head. "No one is getting covered in snow, Phoebe. We will stay safely indoors, which will satisfy the mothers, and still get to play in the snow."

No one looked remotely convinced.

He sighed as patiently as any adult surrounded by uncooperative children is able. "We will be using our imaginations. Like this."

Tugging at his cravat, he slid the fabric free from his shirt and gestured for one of the younger boys to come to him. The tyke did so, torn between confusion and curiosity.

"John, isn't it?" Hugh prodded with a smile.

The boy nodded. "Yessir."

Hugh nodded in return, then draped his cravat around the boy's neck loosely as one might a scarf. "John, you are now a man of snow, as I lay this imaginary scarf upon you."

Obediently, John stared straight ahead and held his arms out at the awkward angles one might have seen in sticks used for such a purpose.

Hugh grinned and looked at the other children. "What else does a proper snowman need?"

"A hat!" one of the girls called, jumping to her feet. "I know where one is!" She dashed out of the room at a surprisingly breakneck pace.

"And a pipe!" Tommy added, darting over to a larger chair in a corner of the library. Or, rather, to the small table beside it, where a well worn, well loved pipe lay. He snatched it up and returned to them. "Come on, John. Clamp it between your teeth as Uncle Dough does."

The children all laughed, and John obediently did so, his lips never once wrapping around the pipe.

"Come now," Hugh said to the rest, gesturing to young John. "Can you not find some pretend stones for buttons or eyes?"

Their imaginations needed no further encouragement, and they began to find all sorts of imagined inanimate objects to use on their pretend snowman. Their cousin returned with someone's top hat and propped it on John's head, where it dwarfed the lad and nearly came down to his ears. He tilted his head back to be able to see the rest, giggling wildly now that his pipe was high in the air.

Hugh chuckled himself and let the children lead the way in the rest of the game, watching fondly as they pretended to build up snow around John to make him increase in size. Even Phoebe giggled incessantly, pretending to mound up armfuls of snow before dancing around in circles, imagining catching snowflakes on her tongue.

"What a mighty fine snowman," Hugh commented after a time. "Shall we build another? What say you?"

The children cheered and John shook himself out of his costume, clearly eager for his turn at building a snowman now.

"Who should be the snowman?" Hugh asked, tapping a finger to his chin and looking around at the gathering. "Hmm."

"You!" Phoebe suggested loudly, surprising him with the force of her answer.

He couldn't manage to hide his shock. "Me?"

She nodded insistently, and the others joined their voices with hers. "Yes! Yes, Mr. Sterling!"

Strangely, Hugh was oddly pleased by the notion. Imagine being wanted by a group of people for anything pleasurable, even if they were all under the age of ten. He hadn't known a feeling like that in some time, and the jolt of pleasure that hit his midsection seemed somehow both foreign and familiar.

He put his hands on his hips, frowning for effect. "But how will any of you reach high enough to do a proper job of it?"

The children looked at each other, frowning in thought, when Amelia suddenly moved to Hugh and tugged on his hand. "Sit down, Mr. Sterling."

He looked at her in mock surprise. "Sit down? What for?"

The girl rolled her eyes dramatically. "You'll be a sitting snowman, silly. Sit!"

Hugh did so without argument, and at once, the pipe was stuck between his teeth, his cravat tossed about his neck. The hat was tilted to one side atop his head, and a serious discussion on strategy commenced, the children tugging at his clothing and pretending to pile snow around his ankles. It was an impressive imagined endeavor, studiously giving the impression of his seated position. Faux buttons and facial features were laid out, though not placed on him yet.

His anticipation knew no bounds.

"What in the world is going on here?"

The prim crispness of the voice made Hugh smirk as he glanced over his shoulder.

Elinor Asheley stood in the doorway, a smile on her face as she took in the children.

The smile vanished as she took in Hugh.

"You!" she cried, her voice now one of dismay. "What are you doing here?"

He gestured to the children's obvious efforts. "Being made into a snowman, as you see."

Elinor's brow wrinkled. "You're… playing with the children?"

"He's so much fun!" at least two of the children cried.

"Is he?" Elinor asked mildly, her expression not changing, spearing him with a look as though he had somehow coerced the children.

Phoebe nodded eagerly and threw her arms around Hugh's neck. "He was a monster, and then a dog, and then a silly dog, and then I said I wanted to go outside, but he said we couldn't, so he taught us how to play with pretend snow inside! Now we get to have fun, *and* Mama won't be cross!"

Somehow, the little girl's enthusiasm managed to crack Elinor's sour look. Elinor smiled with real amusement at the child and came further into the room. "What a fine compromise! And how much snow have we piled upon Mr. Sterling so far?"

The children took great delight in showing her the imagined snow upon him, as well as his hat, scarf, and what would become his face and buttons when the time came.

To her credit, Elinor nodded thoughtfully as they showed her, and she avoided any scowling, snarling, or giving the impression that she was anything less than fascinated by their efforts.

What composure that must have taken.

Impossibly, she actually joined in the game for a few minutes, helping the girls to pack snow around Hugh's torso.

Interesting. She could be this close to him without breaking out into some sort of horrible rash? Would wonders never cease?

"Elinor," Amelia huffed, propping one hand on a hip. "Move Mr. Sterling's arm. It's not sticking out as it should."

Elinor looked at her cousin, then back to Hugh, raising a brow as she smiled rather smugly. "And how should it be, Amelia?"

Hugh gave her a warning look. "Don't you dare," he muttered out of the corner of his mouth.

Her brows quirked in a blatant dare. "Amelia?"

The girl waved her hand dismissively. "Any way, really. We are using sticks for arms, so they should look like sticks."

"Excellent," Elinor practically purred, eyeing his limb in an almost feral manner.

Hugh was wincing before her hands ever touched him.

"Oh, good," he grunted. "Now I'll really feel frozen."

Elinor's eyes narrowed. "Phoebe, do snowmen talk?"

"No, of course not!" came the outraged reply.

"Then perhaps put additional snow where the mouth should be," Elinor suggested as if it would be helpful. "And there will be no need to make a mouth out of stone or vegetable or anything else."

Hugh gave her a disparaging look, and she fought a smile or a laugh as she carelessly, and forcibly, moved his arm over his head to the most awkward angle humanly possible.

He shook his head, keeping his attention on her rather than on any of the children.

Elinor Asheley was a lovely looking woman, no matter how

much of a termagant she made herself to be in nature. The way she looked now, full of laughter and amusement, though it was all at his suffering, gave a greater light to her countenance and a rosier hue to her cheeks. Her eyes were impossibly blue, he could see them clearly when she was this close, and he was positive he had never seen anything to equal them in life or art.

His mind took him back to the night before when she and her sisters had sung for the gathering. Elinor had looked no less lovely then, even when she had been filled with indignation against him. And when she had sung…

He had yet to understand or explain it, but although the four Asheley sisters had remarkably similar voices whether singing or speaking, he had been able to single out Elinor's voice with ease. More than that, he could hear it more than the rest. Above the rest.

In retrospect, he knew that had to have been impossible. The others had spoken of the lovely blend the sisters' voices had been, what a pristine arrangement it was, and that, while none of the Asheley girls had what they would have called impressive voices, together they were incomparable musically. There was no way that one voice ought to have been distinguishable from the rest.

Yet he had heard Elinor.

More than that, he had been struck by Elinor. Her voice had moved him, stunned him, captivated him, beyond anything he had ever known. He had been in the highest circles of Society, had heard voices that had brought others to tears of joy, been privy to performances by the greatest musical talents recognized. Nothing had made him feel as the night before had.

Hers was not the most talented voice his ears had known, but it made no difference.

It was her voice he had heard, and hers that had brought to his heart something he had not known in several months, if not years.

If ever.

Elinor Asheley, of all people.

He refused to really consider what that meant, what significance that might have held, or anything of the sort. Not yet, not in depth, and possibly not ever.

He may not have to.

The warm, sweet scent of orange blossom captured his senses then, and with it a hint of cinnamon and sandalwood, all of which suddenly distracted him from concise thought and sense. What a perfect blend, both enticing and comforting, and it sent ripples of pleasure and alertness across his skin. Where had it come from, and why should it now swamp him so?

Elinor was leaning close, he realized, assisting her young cousin in pretend-patting of snow across his abdomen. He inhaled as faintly as possible, and the scent intensified, magnified if he turned his face more towards her. Instinctively, he did so, suddenly desperate for that fragrance to enfold him as completely as possible.

He couldn't help it; he stared at her. Blatantly, frankly, and without shame. How could he not? Her singing had enchanted him, her appearance fascinated him, and now her scent held him captive. This woman who hated him with all the passion one might save for the devil himself, and now she was holding sway over him?

Somehow, the idea did not distress him so much as make him curious. It was not nearly as distasteful as it would have been only days ago, and he feared the more time he spent in this house, the less distasteful it would grow still.

What a thought.

But then, if such a miraculous change of feelings and opinions could occur, it may yet be possible that Hugh Sterling would not be the villain in the eyes and thoughts of Society as he was at present. And better yet, to the Spinsters themselves.

He had wronged them all in some way, a few individuals more than others, and he would not be in any way opposed to making amends there. If he could somehow be even remotely redeemed by them, he would not feel himself so very beneath decent company.

Elinor might be his way to achieve that. If he could convince her that he was changed, if he could make her hate him less than before, it could go a long way indeed.

He wanted to be changed for Elinor. To Elinor. Not only for the sake of the Spinsters themselves, but for her specifically.

He wanted to be redeemed to her.

Bewildering thought though it was.

"Oh, dear me, look at the time!" Elinor said, glancing up at the clock on the mantle. "Forgive us, dears, but I must take our snowman away. My mother wished us both at luncheon, and I believe your nanny will have some in the nursery for you all."

The children groaned in displeasure, but dutifully filed out of the library, the promise of food no doubt comforting whatever grief the end of their game brought them.

Hugh chuckled as he slid his cravat beneath the collar of his shirt and began to tie it simply, without a looking glass or any real concern.

"I'm amazed you survived such an extensive game of make-believe," Elinor commented drily, pushing up to her feet. "My cousins' children require a great deal of energy."

"They do," Hugh admitted as he continued tying. "Thankfully, I have a great deal of energy of late. Far more than I once did."

Elinor grunted softly, then looked at him, one brow rising. "Do you not need a valet to tie that to your satisfaction?"

Hugh looked at her, smiling. "I possess the necessary skills, have no fear."

She snorted once. "Yes, that was exactly what I feared. I am so distressed."

"So I see." He tucked his cravat in and rose, brushing off the lapels of his coat lightly. "I did not travel with a valet, Elinor. I don't care if my cravat is in fashion, I don't care if the children ask me to play during a quiet moment to myself, and I don't care if your mother's luncheon is nothing more or less than boiled potatoes. I truly, sincerely, do not care."

Elinor stared at him as though she had never quite seen him before. Her expression was not filled with hatred, coldness, or disdain, but curiosity.

He dared not think anything else of it than that, and he did not blame her.

It was a curious change he had undergone; he knew it well.

"I told you, Elinor," he murmured as he gestured for her to lead the way out of the library. "I am not the man I was. Is that so surprising, considering…?"

Elinor surprised him by shaking her head as they walked out of the room. "No, when I put it in the proper light, it's not so surprising. How could any man do any less in your situation? And I am not so heartless as to not consider your words from last night in all sincerity, if not solemnity. I would never wish what happened with your sister upon any young woman or any brothers of one. Not even you."

Hugh glanced at her as they walked side by side now, and a wave of pleasant surprise slowly rolled through him. He whistled very low. "Not even me?" he repeated with humor. "Whatever did it cost you to say that, Elinor?"

She smiled at that, which was the greatest shock of all. "Just a little chip of my pride. It needed to go anyway."

He chuckled at that and smiled towards one of the great windows. "I'm not the great serpent of hell, then?"

"Not today, at least. You're only human." She made a small laughing sound. "But you may have a forked tongue. Of that, I am not entirely sure."

Just to spite her, he turned back and stuck his tongue out as a spoiled child might have. "Well?" he asked around the blockage of his tongue.

Elinor pretended to inspect it, then sighed. "Pity. I shall have to amend my opinions, I see."

She should what?

"Can you?" he asked, no longer teasing, her answer suddenly quite important.

She shrugged a shoulder. "Perhaps. After all, I was quite wrong about Camden Vale. I admit it freely and without remorse. But in your case, it will all depend." She looked up at him. "Tell me this: will you make the necessary apologies when you find yourself in London again?"

"Of course, I will," he informed her without hesitation. "Most sincerely. I've written several letters in my absence, all of which have been sent, begging forgiveness, if it can be given at all. Georgie's had one, as has Mrs. Vale and Mrs. Morton. I believe I have wronged them most among your circle of friends, though all of you deserve my apologies."

"Even me?" she asked, though he detected no hint of insinuation there.

He stopped in the corridor, and so did she. "Yes, Elinor, even you," he said softly. He took one step towards her. "I have no explanation or excuse for my behavior, for my words, or for any harm or hurt I may have caused. I can only offer an apology as deep as a man's regret can be, which, I have found, is beyond comprehension. I pray that someday I might earn your forgiveness, but if I can only have my apology accepted as such, I will be content. I am truly sorry. I hope you can believe that."

Elinor looked at him for a long moment, her expression maddeningly unreadable. "Do you know," she replied quietly, "I believe I can."

Hugh blinked once. "You can what?"

"Believe you," she clarified. "I believe your apology, and I believe you are sincere. More than that, I accept it, whatever that is worth from me."

"Really?" He grinned out of sheer relief. "I didn't expect that."

"Nor did I, believe me," Elinor commented as she began to walk again. "Only an hour ago, I was considering ways to make you fall through the ice."

He hissed a wince as he followed, falling in step beside her again. "I'm a terrible swimmer. Could we not have me somehow strung up by holly and ivy and whatnot?"

"And have you become part of the decor? I think not, we have no greenery to spare for you."

"More's the pity."

"You have no idea."

Chapter Five

There is nothing more dangerous to an unmarried man than a room filled with eligible, desperate, intrepid women. Be ye forewarned.

-The Spinster Chronicles, 13 February 1819

"What's the matter with you, Elinor?"

Elinor looked at her younger sister in surprise. "Nothing is wrong with me, E. Why would you ask?"

Elizabeth raised a trim brow. "You didn't make a single face during supper. You appeared calm and content, and I would swear you even smiled at something that Mr. John Winthrop said."

Clearly, the punch was getting to her sister's head.

"I did smile," Elinor informed her without shame. "It was a witty remark."

"I thought you hated all men," Elizabeth muttered in a low voice, eyes wide. "I've never seen you smile at a single one before."

All men? Well, that was hardly fair. Elinor didn't *know* all men; how could she hate them all? She winced and could have kicked herself. She had gone through a rather violent phase of hating all male creatures, be they horses, humans, or hounds, and none were spared from her barbs. Her friends in the Spinsters would certainly have had the same opinions her sister did, undeserved though they were.

No, that wasn't right. They were deserved, at the time.

When exactly her opinions had changed, she couldn't have said.

She didn't hate Tony Sterling, Georgie's husband, and she didn't hate Camden Vale, Prue's. She was learning to like Sebastian Morton, the man who had married Izzy, though there was not much at all to dislike in him. Grace's husband, Lord Ingram, she already liked immensely.

That had surprised her, considering she hadn't known much about him when he'd crossed their path, but he was almost sinfully handsome, witty in all the best ways, and had a measure of irreverence that made him almost addictively charming. Meeting him had shifted something in Elinor, though she would have to be honest enough to admit that it had begun to shift before then.

If Lord Ingram had had eyes for anyone but Grace, Elinor would have considered tossing her bonnet or handkerchief in his direction.

What a revelation that had been.

Considering the guests they had at Deilingh at the present, the ones she was not indirectly related to, at any rate, she would have to say that she did not hate any of them either.

Not even Hugh Sterling.

She glanced up at the ceiling, half expecting pieces of it to rain down upon her head. All she could see was mistletoe.

Well. *That* was wholly inappropriate.

All she admitted was that she did not hate him.

It did not mean that she particularly liked him. And certainly did not allow for anything remotely resembling mistletoe where he was concerned.

Not unless she could catapult it at him.

She smiled at that idea.

"And now you're smiling," Elizabeth sighed, shaking her head. "Next, you'll be telling me that you find Mr. John Winthrop attractive."

Elinor glanced at her sister, then cast her eyes across the room to the tall, dark, and undeniably handsome brother of their cousin's husband, currently being interrogated by one of her eligible cousins. "I am not blind, E, no matter what my opinions may be. I find him exceedingly attractive."

"Too attractive, one might say," their brother commented as he came up beside them.

Elizabeth chortled and gave Edmund a wry look. "Is there such a thing?"

Edmund nodded firmly, tugging at his starched cravat. "There most certainly is. And you never trust that sort of man, am I right, Sterling?"

"Generally speaking, yes," Hugh replied as he joined them, bowing to Elinor and Elizabeth with a smile. "But I've got a rather poor history when it comes to judgments, so my word is not worth much."

Elinor coughed a laugh, fisting her gloved hand before her mouth to avoid choking on her own breath.

Hugh eyed her with a sly grin. "Something to add, Miss Asheley?"

She shook her head, swallowing with difficulty. "No, not at all. I swallowed poorly, forgive me."

He nodded slowly in understanding. "Swallowing can be a struggle for some, though I do believe one is usually accustomed to the action at a younger age than you can boast."

Elinor narrowed her eyes at him, wondering when he had become so adept at playful teasing.

"For shame, Mr. Sterling," Elizabeth chuckled, having no need to feign her amusement. "One does not discuss a lady's age in polite company."

"Whose age?" Letitia demanded as she suddenly, and insistently, made herself known to their small group. "Not mine, I hope."

Elinor barely restrained a snort. "No, Letitia, not yours. Indeed, we were not discussing you at all."

"Personally, I never do," Edmund admitted freely. "Never."

"No reason to at all," Elizabeth chimed in.

Letitia glared at them all as though they had risen from hell itself. "In some families, you know, there is a measure of respect for each other."

"Hmm," Elinor mused, tapping a finger to her chin. "What would that be like?"

Letitia's upper lip curled in a snarl before transforming into a sickeningly simpering expression as she snaked her hand through Hugh's arm. "Do come and join *our* conversation, Mr. Sterling. It will be a far better use of your time than standing here with these jaded cynics."

She tugged on his arm, leaving no polite way for him to refuse, and he let himself be tugged.

"Jaded cynics, miss?" Hugh echoed in a pained tone, though his pleading expression towards Elinor and her siblings left them in no doubt regarding what he was pained about.

"Aren't you going to save him?" Elizabeth asked softly, giggling to herself.

Elinor shook her head as she waved at Hugh. "Not for the world," she replied.

"What has poor Mr. Sterling done to deserve Letitia's company?" Ellen asked as she practically bounced into the room. "Lord, what a prospect. Are we saving him?"

"No," her siblings replied in the same unconcerned tone, watching their cousin lead their guest to other eager cousins, all vying for any scrap of attention.

It was a comedy that anyone of sense would have found amusing.

"You four are really quite horrible," Uncle Dough remarked. "At least Mr. John has Barbara near him, she's the best of the lot, but Mr. Sterling? Surely he deserves some sort of ally."

"Excuse me," Ellen huffed with all the indignities a girl of fifteen can muster. "I have only just arrived, and I would never subject anyone to Letitia who was not fully apprised of what was coming."

Elinor bit her lip on a giggle, which, somehow, Hugh must have heard, for he glanced up at her, looking as cross as anyone.

Uncle Dough hummed to himself, sipping his glass of Madeira slowly. "And did Mr. Sterling get an apprisal of what was coming?"

"He did not," Edmund said simply. "There wasn't time."

"And Elinor did nothing to stop her," Elizabeth added, as if it would be helpful.

Elinor looked to Uncle Dough with a smirk. "I am not Mr. Sterling's keeper. Perhaps he will find Letitia a charming companion."

There was a pause among the group at the thought.

"I may be ill," Ellen suddenly muttered, leaning against Uncle Dough as though she were faint.

"You're not the only one," their uncle replied.

Elinor burst out laughing, not bothering to cover her mouth. "Uncle Dough! You cannot say such things about your niece!"

"I certainly can," he retorted, puffing out his expansive chest. "I have no qualms about claiming favorites among your generation, and while I may not admit to the identity of those favorites, I will tell you that she has not made the list."

"My poor sister," Lavinia mused as she swept into the room, far and away fairer than her sister, and infinitely more sensible. "She does so want to have a husband, and I don't believe she particularly cares as to his identity."

"Careful, La-la," Uncle Dough warned with a smile, using the pet name she'd borne as a child. "There are too many candidates for the position hereabouts, and they might be of a similar mindset." He gave his niece a careful look. "And you might find one of them more agreeable than the rest yourself."

Lavinia scoffed quietly. "That would be a feat. Next, you'll be telling me Elinor will find one. Or Barbara. Or that one will persuade Lucinda out of the kitchen to socialize." She looked over her shoulder and made a brief chirp of a sound. "Speaking of candidates…" She glanced at the others, her lips quirking into a smile. "Perhaps I shall devote myself to controlling Letitia this evening. 'Twould be a kindness, don't you think?"

"Certainly would," Edmund muttered as their cousin moved to sit decidedly between her sister and Hugh. "Might get her nominated for sainthood."

Elinor could only nod as she watched the irritation flash across Letitia's plain features, and as Mr. Davis and Rigby entered the room, talking with a few cousin husbands with great enthusiasm.

The room would soon be filled with the rest of the adults, and there would barely be room enough to breathe. Her father would ask Fredericka to play something, and with the excess of eligible gentlemen, Letitia would offer to sing.

She would have to save herself from that ordeal, but the particular excuse would need to be right. Her mother greatly disapproved of blatant avoidance, but Elinor and her siblings had always banded together over their escape.

Emma was fortunate enough to have her children for an excuse, but as for the rest…

"What a fine meal!" Elinor's father boasted as he came into the room, his cheeks red already with too much brandy. "I have never had better, I do declare."

"Lord above," Elizabeth grumbled, opening her fan and fluttering it gently. "Who gave Papa brandy?"

"No idea," Uncle Dough grunted, downing his Madeira in one gulp.

"Music!" her father cried, clapping his hands. "Let us have music!"

Edmund groaned and craned his neck. "We had music last night, isn't that enough?"

"Shh!" Ellen hissed, nudging their brother hard. "It's the only night we get to escape. He never lets us leave during cards or theatricals."

"Does he know we leave during the music?" Elinor mused, glancing at her younger sister. "I seem to remember him being quite forgetful when it comes to these things."

Elizabeth rounded on Elinor. "Did *you* give him the brandy?"

Uncle Dough snickered darkly and shook his head. "I am moving to another part of the room. I don't want your actions on my conscience." He bowed to them quickly, then moved to talk with great-aunts Julie and Beatrice.

"Coward!" Elizabeth hissed after him.

Elinor cleared her throat. "So how *are* we escaping Letitia's recital?"

Edmund shrugged a shoulder and tugged at his cravat again. "Like this." He took one final sip of his beverage, set the glass down, then grabbed Ellen's hand and tugged her out of the room without another word.

Elinor and Elizabeth gaped after their siblings, then immediately stood closer together to avoid any sign of gaps.

"I cannot believe he did that," Elizabeth hissed, her cheeks flushing.

"Oh, I can." Elinor watched as, to be expected, Fredericka moved to the pianoforte, Letitia practically at her heels. "Edmund is not known for his tact, and by taking Ellen, he can freely admit he was helping his sister, which will settle Mama's ruffled feathers."

Fredericka began to play, her fingers almost flying across the keys, her attention entirely focused on her music.

No doubt to tune out what was about to happen.

"Do you ever wonder if Fredericka hates this more than we do?" Elinor asked her sister softly.

Elizabeth coughed delicately. "Probably."

Letitia began to sing, her eyes pointedly skirting to every unmarried man in the room, including Walter and Rupert, and somehow, impossibly, each of them avoided looking as though their ears were being tortured.

Rupert actually seemed to be enjoying it, which only proved he must have been deaf as well as dull.

Poor Fredericka looked as though she might burst into tears at any moment, which did not seem very festive at all.

"Whenever you make your escape," Elinor murmured to her younger sister, "see if you can take Fredericka with you. Maybe say one of her girls is asking for her."

"Lovely," Elizabeth said with a nod. "But who will play instead?"

Letitia finished her attempt at a song, and their cousin Mary was idiotic enough to actually shout a word of praise.

"That answers that question," Elizabeth stated rather simply, not bothering to applaud.

"Certainly does."

"Right, this is my cue," her sister murmured, moving gracefully towards Mary's husband.

Elinor watched as Elizabeth spoke softly with the particular cousin husband in question, who nodded repeatedly, patted Elizabeth's hand, then cleared his throat.

"Mary, would you not accompany Letitia for the next? You both sound so accomplished when blended, and Fredericka's fingers must be fatigued after so masterful a performance."

Mary blushed at the comment, and Fredericka was off the bench in less than two seconds, smiling as warmly as humanly possible at her cousin. Elizabeth intercepted her, linked arms, and strolled with her out of the room without a single additional comment being necessary.

"Nicely done, ladies," Elinor said under her breath, shaking her head at the beauty of such an escape.

Now to try for her own.

There was no easy way to do this, she considered as she looked around. Her mother was already glaring at her, having seen what the others had done, so short of fainting dead away...

That was a thought.

But no, if she were to faint, then the music would be disrupted and everyone would fuss, and it would all lead to Elinor being cooped up in her room and subjected to the treatments of the great-aunts, who somehow considered themselves as capable healers at their age.

Letitia's warbling might have been safer.

A startlingly high and off-key note began the next number and Elinor's skin tingled and crawled in distress.

Never mind. Letitia was far and away worse. But that did not mean Elinor would let herself be treated into an actual sickness by her currently punch-guzzling great-aunts.

The trouble with standing near the fringe of the room was that any possible allies were elsewhere, and with her sister already escaping with a cousin, it would be painfully obvious for Elinor to do the same.

Well, experience had taught her that Letitia had at least five songs in her, only one of which would include another person, and she could not endure that much.

She flinched as her deluded cousin attempted another note beyond her range, then craned her neck to try to restore her body to its usual state.

How had Letitia gotten worse in the last year? It was utterly unfathomable.

Even Letitia's mother looked appalled, and Aunt Catherine, as a rule, always thought of, spoke of, and complimented her daughters well. She would never have been so careless as to display a physical reaction to a flaw from one of them. If anyone asked why her expression looked so wan, she would have claimed indigestion and scolded one of her brothers for having Mrs. Larpenteur make the food too rich.

Elinor glanced at Emma, the only one of her siblings still in the room, and it was clear she was attempting a retreat. But Mr. Partlowe, ever concerned about appearances, had his hand over hers in a gesture of fondness, though Elinor was entirely convinced it was a restraining hand rather than a comforting one.

Huzzah for the lack of husband to insist on such suffering for the sake of politeness.

A movement in the center of the room caught her attention, and she immediately began preparing a statement kindly refusing an offer to take a seat, one explaining her current position, and one that would carefully praise her cousin without actually praising anything at all.

Her guard lowered when she saw Hugh Sterling discreetly making his way towards her.

His expression was entirely unreadable as he approached, and, for a moment, she thought he might pass her and leave the room entirely, which likely would have been cause for comment among the cousins later. But then he stopped beside her and turned to face what was apparently supposed to be music.

"Yes?" Elinor asked quietly, keeping her voice low.

"Save me," he murmured as he fixed a polite smile on his face.

Elinor fought a smile herself. "From?"

"You have to ask?" came the hissed reply.

"I do." She nodded as though with great care. "I am no mind reader, sir, and in order to assist you in any way, I will need to know the specifics."

Hugh cleared his throat softly as Letitia butchered a run of notes. "That."

"For shame, Mr. Sterling," Elinor said, quickly losing the battle with her smile. "My cousin is trying her best, and it is quite daunting for a young woman to perform in front of so many."

Hugh glanced down at her. "I concede to her trying her best. I do not fault the effort." He winced as her voice ventured hoarse for a moment before returning to its usual sound. "Only the delivery."

"Welcome to Christmas with my family, sir," Elinor informed him as she reached for the glass her brother had set down, finishing his Madeira in one gulp. "This has become a tradition as much as the greenery is."

"Enduring this has become a tradition?" he asked incredulously. "Good heavens, why?"

Elinor snorted to herself. "Because Letitia doesn't take hints well, and no one has the nerve to tell her outright that she would be better suited to silently sitting and embroidering the lyrics of a song rather than vocalizing them."

The man beside her snickered, covering the sound with a gloved hand. "And yet it would be an apt statement."

Elinor shook her head. "Not really. She embroiders as well as she sings."

"But no one else is harmed by the act," he pointed out. "At this moment, I am being harmed. Please save me."

"How?" Elinor asked with real honesty. "My siblings have abandoned me, and my mother is watching." She indicated her mother, who, sure enough, was fixated on them.

Hugh stunned her by bowing politely in that direction. "Lovely woman. She looks just like you, especially when she scowls."

Elinor jabbed him in the side with an elbow. "I'll not save anything of yours if you don't behave."

He was instantly contrite. "Of course, Miss Asheley. Whatever you say, Miss Asheley. May I ask you to please show me the way to the guest rooms? I fear I am missing one of my cufflinks there, and I have no recollection of the way."

Of all the ridiculous excuses, that was what he would go with?

She gave him a dubious look, but he stunned her by raising his arm to show, true to his word, he lacked a cufflink.

Oh. Convenient, indeed.

She nodded politely, only slightly ashamed. "Of course. Come with me." She nodded at her mother, who warily nodded back.

Turning out of the room, Elinor let her face relax entirely, Hugh only a half-step behind her. "Oh, lord," Elinor groaned as they moved away from the room. "She's so much worse than she used to be."

"I believe it," he replied easily. "I don't mean to disparage any woman, but…"

"It's an abomination," Elinor overrode. "I know." He seemed surprised that she'd said anything, and Elinor shrugged. "This way, you did not disparage her. I did."

Hugh laughed once and clasped his hands behind his back. "So you did. Thank you for saving me."

She only nodded, fidgeting with her gloves. "Now, which room are you staying in? We can take the long route to avoid more of Letitia's singing."

"Considering she informed me she was singing to land a husband," Hugh mused, his tone rife with humor, "that sounds most agreeable."

"She said that?" Elinor bleated, pausing to gape at him.

Hugh nodded. "She did, and she made sure that I, Mr. John, Mr. Davis, and Mr. Rigby could hear. Though I think only the large and perspiring man in the back seemed remotely interested."

Elinor laughed merrily, covering her face. "That would be Rupert, and he's the son of my father's cousin. Letitia doesn't mind, so long as she gets a husband." She moved to the stairs and, rather than ascend them, sat down with a sigh. "I love my family. I do. But occasionally, I forget just what a strange lot we are, and somehow, having guests witness the melee makes everything worse."

"Believe me, I comprehend the feeling," Hugh admitted, coming over to lean near her. "I'm a Sterling, remember? We could populate our own county, if we chose. And not every branch has the sanity of Tony or Francis."

Elinor smirked at the thought and peered up at him. "And what sort of branch were you?"

He shrugged. "Roughly in the middle, but certainly the top half. I'll never be Francis, but I'm not exactly one of the relations to avoid."

"Is Francis the pinnacle, then?" she asked, wondering for possibly the first time about the nature of things between the brothers. Francis, Lord Sterling, was on her list of close to perfect men, and he had proven himself to be a good friend to the Spinsters.

Hugh was nothing like him.

Or so she'd thought.

Hugh gave her a humorless smile. "Isn't he always?"

She was honest enough to admit the truth there and smiled in return. "The lot of a younger sibling, is it not? I am always being compared to Emma, even before she was married. And now…"

"What?" he asked when she did not finish. "Now that she is no longer a spinster, you must follow the same path?"

"More or less, yes." She shook her head and clasped her hands before her, slouching a little. "The matrimonial part wasn't mentioned for quite a while, for obvious reasons. Now that she has married and borne children, I am suddenly to be found wanting." She rolled her eyes, laughing slightly. "Emma was never to be found wanting at my age, but there it is."

Hugh stared at her, his expression just as inscrutable as before. "What could be found wanting in a young woman enjoying herself in a healthy, proper manner? Or have you really sworn off men entirely, as they say?"

Elinor bit her lip, her laugh now not quite as forced. "I have not, though I was close at times. I am not quite as violent in my spinsterly passion as I was before. I am sure that gives relief to some."

Wisely, Hugh did not respond except to shrug. "I couldn't say. I haven't had association with any in London for some time now."

"Were you not headed to London?" she found herself asking, truly curious.

He shook his head. "Oxfordshire, actually. Francis and Janet are at the family house this Christmas and invited me to join them. I thought to refuse, but then I had a letter from Alice…" He smiled almost wistfully. "I find that I have reached the point where my shame is dwarfed by my desire to see them, and I found myself in a carriage before I fully comprehended what that would mean."

Elinor grinned at that. "Traveling in the winter does tend to require some preparation."

"Now you tell me," he replied, flashing a quick smile in her direction before he sobered again. "I'm not entirely sure how I will be received, but if I cannot come home repentant at Christmas, I may never be able to."

"Oh, I don't know about that," Elinor commented, rubbing her hands together absently. "They wouldn't have invited you if they wanted you away, not if I know Francis. And Alice seems a rather genuine girl, I doubt she would pretend to want you back if she felt otherwise. I'd say you could return repentant at any time and be well received."

Hugh hummed once. "You think so?"

"I do," she confirmed with a nod. Then she smiled more broadly at him. "You may make it in time for the birth even with the delay."

Hugh returned her smile with one equally as grand. "I confess, the prospect of my impending uncle status did sway me a little."

"Don't expect family connections to make you a godparent," she warned as she got to her feet. "My sister had twins, and I wasn't named godmother for either."

He tsked sympathetically. "There is always next time, I suppose."

"If I agree," she retorted. "I may not." She brushed at her skirts and sighed. "Now, which room are you in? We must fetch your cufflink and return, or a search party will hunt you down."

Hugh grinned rather slowly and rather slyly, then reached into a pocket, pulled out a handkerchief, and within was the cufflink.

Elinor stared at it, then flicked her gaze up at him with a laugh. "You are unbelievable!"

He shrugged and held the cufflink out for her to fasten. "I needed a legitimate excuse to flee. *Voila*."

She shook her head and fastened his sleeve, then she stood and smiled. "I applaud your ingenuity. I think we may be safe to return, but perhaps you could request dancing? Mary really is furiously talented, and it would liven up the gathering."

"I shall do my best. Would you dance with me?" he queried, walking beside her. "Or do you still think me venomous?"

Elinor barely avoided biting her lip again. "I don't know…" She suddenly reached for the mistletoe she had hidden the day before and lobbed it at Hugh's head.

"What in the world?" he demanded on a laugh, barely ducking in time.

She burst out laughing, wrapping her arms around her midsection. "I have been wanting to do that for *ages*!"

Hugh shook his head and picked up the offending plant, looking at it before returning his attention to her. "Now that you have cursed me, I believe you owe me a dance, Miss Asheley. It's only fair, as I may sprout horns at any moment."

Still giggling, Elinor nodded. "One can only hope, but I shall keep a weather eye open for my own safety." She inhaled deeply and sighed with satisfaction. "I feel so free at this moment. Yes, Mr. Sterling, let's dance."

His smile made her stomach flip just a little as he bowed, gesturing for her to lead the way. "Let us indeed, Miss Asheley."

Chapter Six

It is entirely unclear what a party of gentlemen discuss whilst engaging in the hunt. It is even more unclear why such a sport is still engaged in during the winter months. What could possibly be pleasant about shooting in the snow?

-The Spinster Chronicles, 9 January 1819

Hugh whistled a rather jaunty rendition of *Adeste Fidelis* as he worked at his cravat, letting the knot be a bit haphazard. Generally, he did his best to make a good impression, but he had felt so comfortable of late with the family, and with his surroundings, that he did not mind leaving things a bit more casual.

Comfortable. What a concept.

He hadn't been comfortable in ages. Even before his self-imposed banishment, he could not say he had been comfortable.

Ignorant, perhaps. Slothful, certainly. Self-indulgent, absolutely.

Comfortable, never.

Three days here, and he was almost perfectly at ease.

Almost, because a certain young woman he had spent a deal of time raging against and avoiding as though she guarded the gates of hell itself was becoming the person he sought out. Someone who could make him laugh. Someone who brought a smile to his face just by entering the room.

It was enough to make a man question everything in his life, but he really did not care to think about it all that much.

Imagine anyone trying to comprehend how Hugh Sterling found himself growing ever more attracted to Elinor Asheley, and not just because of her physical appearance.

He shook his head now, still whistling.

No one would understand.

He didn't understand, but he was rather enjoying it all the same.

The coach would likely be mended and ready for departure today, but, if he were to be honest, he would have admitted he was loath to leave. He was enjoying himself, and there was nothing that said he needed to be with his family on Christmas Day, particularly if they were unaware that he would be coming. He could get there by Twelfth Night and still be festive.

If he wished to be festive.

The Asheley family, and their extended cohorts, were a warm and inviting bunch, even the desperate spinster cousins. Or cousin, he supposed. After dancing with each of the eligible cousins, including Lucinda, he would have to say that only Letitia was desperate. Lucinda's conversation had been purely on food and cuisine, Lavinia had been droll, Barbara had stammered, and Letitia… Well, she had been attempting flirtation, which had made him exceedingly uncomfortable.

He could only be grateful they had kept to more lively dances and avoided anything resembling or related to a waltz.

Elinor had laughed at him the entire time, including their two dances together.

Two.

He almost never danced with the same woman twice, preferring a variety of partners to any repetitions, but last night had been an exception.

One he'd rather liked.

Time would tell if they would dance together again, let alone multiple times in a night. He would need to have a care for her reputation, and being surrounded by her family meant suspicions would reign twice as high, but surely…

He stopped whistling and paused by the stairs. He realized he was already planning on multiple dances with her, no matter what hesitant speculation was going on in his mind. As he understood it, there was to be a formal ball in a few evenings, the night before Christmas Eve, and the family were making plans to invite any and all neighbors, as well as seeing that the house was suitably trussed up.

He would dance with Elinor then, to be sure, and would easily get away with multiple dances in a night when the numbers would be so increased.

It was the smaller, improvised dances where he would need to take care.

Provided she actually consented to dance with him. Elinor was exactly the spirited type that would refuse him on a principle, and even on a whim. She had no qualms about throwing the polite practices of Society to the wind and thought nothing of the consequences. She knew precisely what she was doing at any given time and saw no need to be anything less than herself.

She would not have been as easily persuaded into behavior that others would frown upon or do anything that would make her family ashamed. She was far too strong to be turned in such a way, to be swayed as he had been.

Elinor Asheley was made from sterner stuff than Hugh Sterling, and that was the truth.

In a shocking turn of events, he would be forced to admit that he did not deserve her.

Not that he had her, or had plans for such, or anything of the sort, but if it should ever come up, he did not deserve her, and he knew it.

What a revelation!

Hugh exhaled with some difficulty, feeling he might need to ponder on the subject a bit more in private in order to truly comprehend the change.

This woman hated him. Had raged against him. Would have damned him to hell, had she the power to do so.

Yet she hadn't flinched at seeing him in at least thirty hours. She had not sneered after his outbursts that first night, and, aside from her antics during his time as a snowman, she'd really not been up to any mischief where he had been concerned.

He didn't count her throwing mistletoe at him. He'd actually found that rather charming.

Amazingly enough.

He smiled at the memory, and continued down the stairs, rounding the balustrade and heading for the breakfast room.

The Asheleys, he had learned, were rather relaxed when it came to breakfast. Most of the ladies took trays, but a few were intrepid enough to venture down to partake with the men.

Elinor was among them.

She met his eyes as he entered and immediately smiled just a touch as she brought her tea to her lips.

Hugh let himself watch her do so, fascinated by the play of her lips, and how full they were. He'd never paid much attention to lips, really, but something about Elinor's when they smiled was perfection.

She widened her eyes at him, and he jerked, wrenching his gaze away and striding for the open seat at the far end of the table. Quickly filling his plate, he focused on the task of enjoying the meal without doing anything to draw comment or give anyone insight into his thoughts.

"Hungry, Mr. Sterling?"

Hugh bit back a groan, but carefully dabbed the corner of his mouth with the linen serviette, looking up at the woman he had unwittingly sat beside.

Elizabeth Asheley.

The spit of her eldest sister with the fire of her elder sister, and he had yet to determine where her good sense lay along the paradigm of young ladies.

He smiled with what he hoped was polite warmth. "Always, Miss Elizabeth, especially at breakfast."

"E," her brother scolded as he took the seat across from her, "commenting on a person's appetite is impolite. Would you like Mr. Sterling to ask after yours?"

Elizabeth shrugged easily. "Why not? I have one, after all."

Hugh took a bite of ham, chewed carefully, then asked, "How is your appetite, Miss Elizabeth? Is it in good health?"

Someone down the table coughed a laugh, and he suspected it might have been Elinor.

Elizabeth smiled tightly, her eyes dancing with restrained laughter. "What a polite phrasing, Mr. Sterling. Yes, thank you, my appetite is quite well. It is always quite well."

Hugh nodded in acknowledgement. "I should hope it is well, Miss Elizabeth. And if I may say, you appear none the worse for wear because of it."

Elizabeth returned his nod primly and replied by taking an extra-large bite of her potatoes.

"Lovely, E," Edmund snorted as he buttered a scone. "Really, quite ladylike."

Hugh bit into his own scone, then gave the young woman a questioning look. "E?" he repeated. "Why do they call you E? Surely that must be confusing for the rest."

"One would think so," Elizabeth managed around the remnants of her potato. "But when I was small, it seemed my parents had difficulty remembering which name belonged to me. In an attempt to remedy the oversight, they began to call me simply E." She batted her lashes playfully. "I learned to reply." She snorted softly and returned to her breakfast. "You can imagine how much worse things got when Ellen came around. Yet somehow, her name is never forgotten…"

Edmund chortled, wiping at his mouth with the serviette. "And Elizabeth never fails to remind us all of that fact whenever it seems relevant."

The siblings gave each other simpering smiles, and Hugh had the distinct impression that Elizabeth kicked her brother under the table.

Oddly enough, the action made him miss his brother and sister with a sudden sharpness.

"Edmund, do make haste," Mr. Asheley boomed as he rose from his seat and sidled towards the door. "And Mr. Sterling, you as well, sir. We mustn't be late for the hunt. Mr. John, sir, do join us."

Edmund jumped up from his seat, shoving the rest of his scone in his mouth, taking no care for the politeness of it. He immediately strode from the room, clapping his father on the shoulder.

John Winthrop and Hugh exchanged surprised glances, and Hugh looked at Elinor. "Is it not too cold for the hunt?"

Elinor smiled slyly. "Not at all. It's tradition, Mr. Sterling. Just bundle up, you'll be fine."

He wrinkled up his nose at the thought. "Never been much of a sportsman myself."

Now she laughed. "Don't say that too loudly. Uncle Dough and Uncle Jones will take you under their wing, and then Mr. Perry will recite every psalm and proverb about God's creations that he knows."

"There are quite a few," Elizabeth chimed in, taking a rather dainty bite of toast.

"And the cousin husbands always invent a competition between them," Elinor added, sipping her tea again. "Mr. Layton never wins, but Mr. Tyson, Mr. Clarke, and Mr. Burley-Pratt get quite vocal about the whole affair."

Hugh blinked at her, trying to comprehend. "And Lord Winthrop?"

"Wins every year," they recited together.

It was madness. Absolute madness, the sheer number of people that were in this house.

He shook his head. "That is a fair number of men on a hunt."

Elinor laughed rather darkly. "Oh dear, Mr. Sterling. All the men of the family go on the hunt. And all guests. You'll be quite surrounded, and I fear all the ones related to us are quite nosey when it comes to guests. Do warn the others, won't you?" She smiled what should have been a sweet smile, but it churned his stomach uncomfortably.

He'd opened his mouth to retort when the butler came to the door and bowed. "Mr. John, Mr. Sterling, if you gentlemen would be so good as to follow me."

There was nothing for it, then.

Hugh rose, shaking his head and glaring at Elinor.

She waved her fingers almost merrily at him.

"And what will you be doing?" he demanded.

"We'll be ice skating," she informed him. "If we don't sneak over to watch."

Oh lord, the very idea.

Elinor waved him farewell again, and this time he left, following the somber-faced butler without another word.

"I'm afraid I'm not suitably dressed for the hunt, Hopkins," Hugh admitted with a sheepish smile. "Not much of a sportsman."

"Not to worry, sir," Hopkins replied in a completely unconcerned tone. "The family is quite accustomed to such occasions. There's an excess of coats and scarves and the like set aside for such things. I've had the footmen fetch your own coat and hat, sir, and anything else you might need will be provided."

Well, there went that excuse.

Hugh hummed softly in thought. "I take it the family values this particular tradition, Hopkins."

The butler nodded as he gestured to the footmen to help Hugh with his coat and hat. "Indeed, sir. Mr. James and Mr. George never miss an opportunity to have the Christmas hunt, and were Mr. Asheley here, he'd be part of it, too."

"That's Howard Asheley, yes?" Hugh queried as he shrugged into his coat, his mind racing through the ridiculous number of names he was tasked with keeping straight for the time being.

"Yes, sir."

Hugh exhaled, looking towards the path to the gamekeeper's cottage where the other men were gathering. "Any advice, Hopkins?"

The butler raised one dark eyebrow. "On what, Mr. Sterling?"

"Keeping them all straight," he suggested, his mouth curving slightly. "Topics of conversation. Managing to maintain a good impression if I'm a terrible shot."

Impossibly, the butler seemed to chuckle. "Don't address anyone by name, keep to festive themes, and be relatively self-deprecating. That should keep you safe, sir."

Hugh stared at the butler in shock, wondering if the lines at the man's eyes were actually from restrained laughter rather than stoic disapproval. "Hopkins, you are a treasure of untold wealth."

"Thank you, sir," Hopkins replied with an almost cheeky bond. He gestured for the door, seeming to smile a bit more fondly.

Nothing for it, then. Hugh bit back another heavy exhale and trudged his way out into the snow.

The gamekeeper's cottage was not far, which was another unusual feature of the estate, though it was hardly strange. In fact, at the moment, he was quite pleased it was so close.

Trudging through snow had never been a particular fondness of his.

"Ah, Sterling," the one they called Uncle Dough said, grinning with warmth. "Come to engage in this mess, are you?"

"For my sins, yes," Hugh admitted, nodding to the few others who had noticed his approach. He drew closer to the large man and rubbed his hands together against the cold. "I'll admit it, sir. I'm a terrible shot."

Uncle Dough chuckled heartily and patted him soundly on the back. "Not to worry, lad. You'll find that most of us are poor shots, but the worst shot of all is Rupert there." He indicated the beefy, red-faced younger man currently holding a rifle as though it were a grand walking stick of sorts.

It was the most inane spectacle he'd ever seen.

Which was saying a great deal.

There was no recourse but to shake his head. "Is it wise to give him a firearm, sir?"

"Of course not," came the chortled reply. "But it's a far cry safer than giving one to Walter." He gestured to a scrawny, timid, almost skittish-looking man with the same looks as the other, only appearing to be rather starved by comparison.

Hugh watched as one of the cousin husbands said something to him, and the man twitched and crossed himself before responding.

"I can see that," Hugh muttered.

"You feel better now, don't you?"

Hugh grinned at the older man. "I do, indeed."

Again, he was thumped on the back. "Good. Stick with me, Sterling. We'll get through this."

That seemed a strange thing to say, but he had no opportunity to ask about it, as the gamekeeper and his lads appeared with the hounds, and they were off to begin the hunt.

Which, as it turned out, was more of simply shooting at grouse and pheasant that the dogs scared out of hiding places.

Hugh probably ought to have known such a thing, but his claim of not being a sportsman was not an idle one. He truly could only count the number of activities out of doors he had participated in on one hand.

Including this one.

"You can fire that gun, can't you, son?" Uncle Dough asked, his tone rife with amusement as he handed his gun off for reloading.

Hugh cast a hard look at him. "Of course." Then his expression broke for a sheepish grin. "Though it would likely be around fifteen years since I have done so, and the first time I've had permission."

"Gads, Sterling," John Winthrop laughed, coming over to stand beside him. "We can remedy that straightaway."

The two of them gave him a brief tutorial on the thing, taking care not to bring attention to his lack of experience, which was not difficult, as the forewarned competition among cousin husbands had already begun.

And Rupert had already injured one of the gamekeeper's lads. Not seriously, but enough that it ought to be noted.

With the help of his instructors, Hugh managed to successfully aim, fire, and eventually shoot one of the birds, which seemed a miracle worthy of celebration, though he would keep that opinion to himself in light of the ongoing competition just down the field.

Not wanting to taint the moment of his success with repeated failures, he set the gun aside after his victory and watched the rest of them.

Uncle Dough was quick to do the same.

Hugh smiled as the man stood beside him. "You don't need to keep me company, sir. Please, continue to shoot, if you'd like."

"I would not like, as it happens," Uncle Dough informed him, folding his arms and watching the others as though he had been named a judge in the competition. "Can't abide shooting myself."

That was not something Hugh had expected to hear, especially after the lengths the man had gone to in instructing Hugh in his own shooting.

He stared at Uncle Dough, mouth gaping slightly. "Why didn't you say something before? I told you I was no sportsman, and if you don't care for shooting either..."

Uncle Dough shrugged, chuckling in an irritatingly knowing way. "It's tradition, man. Once a year, I overcome my aversion to shooting for the sake of being with family. I keep my mouth shut and quietly shoot a round or two, then the thing is done." He eyed Hugh, still smiling wryly. "If you paid any attention, Sterling, you would have seen that I don't aim with any care. Simply shoot in the general direction, and I appear to participate without having to do much."

"Genius," Hugh murmured, shaking his head in appreciation.

"You've mastered an art form."

"I've had a few years to perfect it," came the amused reply. "I find more entertainment in the observation of the others than the action itself."

They watched in silence for a moment, and soon both of them were laughing to themselves at the antics of the others, for good or ill. Some were excellent shots but had terrible tempers, some were good-natured despite being miserable shots, and some were completely frustrated the whole way through, regardless of outcomes.

Elinor's father and uncle were in good spirits for the whole of it, which Hugh was beginning to sense was simply their way. He'd only been among them for a few days, but among his hosts he had yet to see anything but generosity of spirit and cheerful countenances. The extended family held a variety of expression and natures, as evidenced by Mr. Perry currently reciting some proverb or other quite loudly, but the brothers Asheley were never anything less than warm and content.

"Your family seems to be full of the best sort of spirit, Uncle Dough," Hugh heard himself murmur with a smile.

"Feel free to just call me Dough," the older man replied, exhaling a cloud of fog in the cold air. "Or Donald, even, if you want to know. I don't think anybody in the family remembers that, as I have been Dough since the first of the children were little."

Hugh laughed easily. "What a name to have earned!"

Dough shrugged his broad shoulders. "You earn all sorts of names from children, Sterling, as you will come to discover yourself one day."

"Fairly soon, actually," Hugh replied, finding himself smiling. "My brother's wife is due to be delivered of the first of their children directly."

"Prepare yourself for the creativity of children," Dough told him as he turned with a broad smile. "It's a marvelous source of amusement."

Hugh nodded at that. "I will keep that in mind. Now, where do you fit in among the siblings?"

"I'm not."

"Not what?" Hugh asked with a frown.

"A sibling," Dough clarified, his eyes twinkling in the winter light. "I am not sibling to George, Howard, James, and Catherine. I'm a cousin, actually. And a rather obscure one. At least one time removed, and the exact family line is a bit muddled. We tend not to discuss it, as it only confuses the lot of us."

Interesting, indeed. Elinor was rather fond of her uncle Dough, he could safely say, and for him to not only not be a direct uncle, but also a more obscure relative than could be explained easily?

Sounded rather like the mass of confusion that was the Sterling family, actually.

Hugh began to chuckle at memories, names, and faces he had not considered in months, if not years. Cousins and extended relations that had been part of his childhood, but rarely in his adulthood, all forming distinct impressions in his life. They'd never shared holidays together, he could say that safely, but every now and then, they would gather at the largest estate in the family, wherever that happened to be at the time, and raise all manner of hell and confusion in the most enjoyable ways.

"Amused by us, are you?" Edmund Asheley asked as he came over, a polite smile on his face. "We are a comical gathering, I'll allow."

"Actually, I was thinking about my own family," Hugh told the man, who was only a year or so younger than his own age. "There's a great lot of us, and exact connections are unclear for the most part."

Edmund made a face of consideration, nodding at his answer. "Yes, that would be us, as well."

"Certainly would be," Dough grunted by way of reply.

A burst of laughter could be heard in the distance, and Hugh turned towards it, curious. "What was that?" he asked of the others.

"The ladies," Dough told him. "Ice skating, I believe. Another activity I do not engage in."

"For which we are all grateful," Edmund quipped without missing a beat.

Dough cuffed his nephew with a laugh. "Rascal."

John Winthrop looked in the direction of the laughter with a speculative expression. "Do all the ladies skate, Asheley?"

"Most of them," Edmund informed him, shouldering his rifle

with a grin. "The more proper of my female relations remain indoors, but all of my sisters do. And as for my cousins, Barbara, in particular, enjoys the activity."

John's expression remained the same, but he nodded firmly. "I rather enjoy it, as well. If I will not be missed, might I proceed there now that I have done shooting?"

"Of course." Edmund nodded, gesturing towards the obvious path. "Take Davis with you, if you will. There are plenty of ladies that will require the arm of steady gentlemen while on the ice."

John ignored this comment, but did take Davis, as well as his brother, Lord Winthrop, down the path.

Hugh watched them go, then turned to Edmund with a grin. "You knew how to spur him on, didn't you?"

Edmund lifted a shoulder in a careless shrug. "It was a guess, to be sure, but I had some idea. Barbara is my favorite cousin, and it seems Mr. John Winthrop doesn't consider a bluestocking to be such a poor candidate for his affections. I'll leave the speculating to the ladies, but…"

"Well done, lad," Dough praised with a laugh. "Well done, indeed."

There was another burst of female laughter, and it made Hugh smile all the more broadly.

Edmund groaned, shaking his head. "That would be Elinor. No doubt Elizabeth or Ellen have fallen on the ice, and she finds entertainment in their injury."

"Too harsh," Dough reprimanded. "You laugh when they fall, too."

"But I'm a brother," Edmund pointed out. "It's different."

Hugh let the two men debate the topic while his ears strained for another peal of that laughter, whatever caused it.

As if he had willed it into existence, the laughter came again, this time joined by others. But he only heard hers, just as it had been with their singing that first night.

He only heard Elinor, and it made him smile all the more.

Chapter Seven

One may find a friend in the oddest of places, and at the most convenient times. It is advised that you cling to such friends and keep them close.

-The Spinster Chronicles, 25 February 1817

The ladies were all rosy-cheeked for some time after their traditional ice-skating excursion, but no one's cheeks held more color than Barbara, who also had not stopped smiling since Mr. John Winthrop joined them on the ice.

Even looking at her cousin now, Elinor herself was quite simply full of smiles.

She had never seen Barbara looking like this, but no man had ever paid Barbara the sort of attention that Mr. John was, and everyone was beginning to notice.

Especially Letitia.

Glares had never been so potent in this family.

"D'you know, I'm becoming quite fond of that pairing," Ellen told her in a matter-of-fact manner, as she usually did. The girl flopped down onto the couch beside Elinor and sighed. "I think he should propose straightaway."

Elinor coughed a faint laugh. "Do you, Elle? It's only been a couple of days, and all we know is they appear to be fond of each other."

Ellen gave her a dark look. "Barbara is smiling like it's her birthday and she's received a pony. Mr. John is continuously fascinated by whatever she says, which is a rarity, and he had her arm the entire time she skated. If they're not perfectly paired, I despair of all marriages."

"Careful," Elinor warned, smiling fondly at her cheeky sister, so much like herself. "The family will call you either a matchmaker or a marriage cynic."

"Oh, what, like you?" Ellen scoffed loudly, not having a care at all if anyone else heard her. "Absolutely ridiculous. Barbara's a spinster, anyone would say it, but no one ever despaired of her. Not particularly fair to you, is it? You're not a spinster by age, but everyone despairs of you."

Barbara instantly went red, her eyes wide, and she stiffened at suddenly being involved in the conversation by association.

The humor Elinor had been feeling faded at once. "Ellen…"

"I don't understand it at all," her sister went on, her voice rising. "I adore the Spinsters and their Chronicles, and one can hardly claim they are improper when four have married excellent men. Not to mention Emma snatching Partlowe."

"Steady on," Partlowe replied, the color fading from his cheeks.

Emma did not look any better as she bounced one of her twin daughters on her knee. "Ellen."

"What?" Ellen asked, looking around at the room. "Tell me I'm wrong."

"You are wrong," Cousin Joan replied simply, giving her youngest cousin a pitying look. "There is a great difference between Barbara's situation and Elinor's."

"Explain that, if you please," Ellen stated primly, even as her eyes flashed.

"Please don't," Elinor murmured, glancing over at Barbara, who shared a petrified look with her.

The room was silent, waiting for the continuation of what had started out as a quiet conversation between sisters, but was now a full family discussion.

And not a pleasant one at that.

"It's quite simple, dear," Joan began, her pitying smile spreading into outright condescension. "Barbara is exceptionally intelligent. She has a brilliant mind and is well educated. A bit plain, perhaps, but so are we all."

Elinor glanced at Barbara again, and her poor cousin had lowered her eyes to the floor, her ears the color of holly berries.

Mr. John Winthrop didn't look much better, his eyes on the window, his arms stiff by his side.

"But Barbara is not to be faulted for that," Joan went on, her tone becoming almost sing-song in nature. "The right sort of man will find her educated mind charming. Elinor, on the other hand…"

Joan broke off to give Elinor a despairing look.

Elinor wanted to glare back. She ought to have. She was used to fighting for herself and being bold in doing so. She had no qualms about expressing her opinions, letting her face express every emotion she felt, polite or not. Her entire relationship with the Spinsters had been built on such a thing, and her family had dealt with her much longer.

But she could do nothing. Say nothing. Show nothing.

Shame filled her, followed quickly by embarrassment. She did not want Hugh to hear this. He'd spent so long railing against the Spinsters and actively working against them in any respect; what if bringing them up again in this context forced him to reveal some of those same feelings? She would lose the image of him that had been building the last few days. An image she had come to grow especially fond of.

She swallowed hard and forced herself to be as composed as possible in the face of her cousin's accusations.

"Elinor," Joan said again, "has thrown away her reputation and chances at a good match by her association with the Spinsters. A group of unmarried women, who maintained such a status for their own ends, who flaunted their opinions and precarious positions as though it were some flag of misguided independence."

She looked around the room for support, and found several nodding heads, mostly of the ladies, though a few obedient husbands did the same.

Joan nodded an affirmation to them all. "It makes no difference that some of them have married now, as those husbands clearly are doing so in order to attempt a reining-in of their actions. Poor, deluded men, too weak to restrain them from continuing to write such damaging, scurrilous sheets. It has all come to naught." Joan looked directly at Elinor again, her expression now cold. "You will never, ever manage a good, decent, acceptable match while you maintain such poor connections, Elinor. While you seem determined to remain unmarried, it would be unwise to express your opinions to any young ladies equally unattached."

"I beg your pardon?" Ellen blurted, horrified at their cousin's words.

Elinor covered her sister's hand, squeezing tightly.

"You will be poisoned by her words, Ellen," Joan insisted, maintaining a superior tone. "Do not look to her for an example, I beg you."

Ellen stirred beneath Elinor's hold, but Elinor only held her more firmly. "Hush," she whispered to her. "It will serve no purpose."

"You will forgive me, Mrs. Ramsay, for offering a contradictory opinion," a stern, male voice broke into the silence, "but I fear I must."

Elinor looked over at him at once, struck by the perfection in his faint curls, almost the color of toffee, and his strong, proud figure standing before the gathering. He looked the part of a perfect gentleman, his clothing pristine. He held a glass of Madeira in one hand, the other tucked into the pocket of his waistcoat. If it weren't for the stern set of his jaw, he would have appeared perfectly cordial.

His tone said otherwise.

"Please, Mr. Sterling," Joan replied in surprise, gesturing for him to go on.

He nodded politely, despite still looking disgruntled. "Have you ever met the Spinsters, madam? Personally?"

Joan's eyes widened, then she swallowed and shook her head. "No, sir. And I've no wish to, frankly."

"That is much to your detriment, if I may be equally frank," Hugh replied, his tone clipped but in no way rude. "I have been acquainted with almost every one of them for several years at this point. I cannot pretend to have always agreed with them, or even thought well of them, but I can tell you that if I had paid more attention, had more sense than folly, and seen them for the intelligent, considerate creatures they are, my sister might have been spared a near-disastrous experience that will haunt me for the rest of my days."

The room was utterly silent at this stunning announcement, and Elinor, for one, was transfixed on Hugh, nearly breathless for a multitude of reasons she didn't dare comprehend.

"But beyond that," Hugh went on, "I can tell you for a fact that the women with whom Elinor, and I might remind you Mrs. Partlowe, have chosen to associate with, are of the very best you will find in London society. They care for one another rather than compete with one another, they never hesitate to aid someone in need, and they have been courageous enough to find an unconventional way to bring wisdom, entertainment, and hope to others in England. My sister being among them." He tilted his head in inquiry. "You praise Miss Barbara Asheley for independence of mind, yet you condemn Miss Elinor Asheley for the same. They express that independence in different ways, yet their marriage state is the same. I question the scale on which these rulings have been made."

Joan's face was turning an uncomfortable shade of red, and others in the room were now averting their gaze, though none moved from their places.

It seemed that Hugh would be able to make whatever sermon he wished without interruption or contradiction.

How mysterious were the twists of fate.

Hugh turned then to look at Elinor, and his expression somehow softened, yet became more determined.

She couldn't have looked away even if she had tried.

She didn't try.

Didn't want to.

"And in my admittedly limited experience," he murmured, his voice lowering, "Elinor could not associate with a more worthy circle of women, and she is well worthy of them in every respect. Miss Ellen would do well to emulate any of her sisters, including Elinor."

Lord, he could have asked her to marry him in that moment, and she would have accepted, fully and freely.

Somehow, he must have known that, seen that. If not that,

specifically, then at least that her heart had entirely blossomed for his picking. His smile told her he knew something had changed, and that he was quite pleased by whatever he saw.

She smiled at him in return, her heart warming and sending a beacon towards him that would have drawn her close had she any power to move.

"Beyond all of that," Hugh murmured, his eyes darkening in a tempting manner, his smile forming adorable creases at the corners of his eyes, "one of the Spinsters has married my cousin, Captain Sterling. I have grown to respect and admire Georgiana, Mrs. Ramsay, and her position in my family has only improved us, I can assure you. My cousin is a most fortunate man, and a wise one."

Joan fidgeted in her seat, Elinor could see it out of the corner of her eye, but she dared not look away from Hugh.

Hugh, who was stealing her breath and her ability to think.

Hugh, who had sent the most pleasant jolts of heat into the tips of her fingers and the arches of her feet.

Hugh, who made her lips tingle in anticipation of… something…

She exhaled a stuttering breath, not entirely sure when she had inhaled.

Lord, he was handsome.

And that was a paltry thought indeed.

"I do apologize, Mr. Sterling," Joan all but whispered, seeming to tremble where she sat. "I had no idea that… that your family… That you were so connected with them. I meant no offense to you or to your family, certainly."

Hugh's smile turned a touch ironic, and he slowly drew his gaze away from Elinor to glance at Joan. "I mention my family only for context, Mrs. Ramsay, not out of offense. My concern in this matter centers on Elinor and the views her family holds of her. It is she who deserves any apologies you might wish to offer, though I daresay she expects none."

Elinor bit her lip hard, biting back a laugh that would not help anyone at all.

Hugh surprised her further still by turning to Barbara and bowing. "Miss Asheley, if you would be so good as to show me to the library, I would be honored to have a recommendation from you on what I might read during my unoccupied hours here."

Barbara looked surprised, but beamed quite freely up at him, her almost awkward brown ringlets seeming to dance a jig as she rose. "I would be p-pleased to, Mr. Sterling."

"Winthrop, weren't you wishing for a good book yourself?" Hugh asked, giving Mr. John a pointed look.

No man had ever smiled with such luminescence in history. John Winthrop leapt to his feet, nodding excessively. "By Jove, you have an excellent memory, Sterling. Do let us be off, then. I've a fiendish desire for a good book."

The three of them left the room without much of a word, and Elinor fought down a desperate fit of giggles. A "fiendish desire" for a book? John Winthrop either knew the exact way to Barbara's heart or he was the most unexpected scholar on the planet.

And Elinor was well aware that Hugh knew full well where the library was, as he had played with the children there only yesterday.

But that would remain her secret, as his actions were blessedly heroic under the present circumstances. No need to disillusion the company or Barbara.

The room remained silent for a moment, and then Lavinia, without any hesitation, said, "Well, I feel rather an idiot, don't you all?"

Ellen snorted loudly once. "I don't, but I'd wager Joan does."

"Ellen," Elinor choked out, her restrained laughter beginning to make her chest ache.

"What?" her sister asked with all the innocence of a fifteen-year-old.

Elinor only shook her head, feeling rather fond of her impetuous sister, despite her shortcomings.

"I'd like to hear that apology Mr. Sterling mentioned," Mr. Partlowe said almost as an afterthought.

Elinor wrenched her gaze to her usually stoic, propriety-focused brother-in-law, staring at him as though she had never seen him before.

He met her gaze with the fondest smile she had ever seen him bear. "I believe Elinor deserves it."

"So do I," Emma replied, glaring at Joan with a fierceness that would make any sister proud. "After all, the women you rage against, Joan, were my friends before they were hers. I wonder how you spoke about *me* before I married."

"I'm not the only one with these opinions," Joan protested, flinging her arm out to include a majority of the others. "Any one of the others could have said the same."

"True," Elinor murmured, speaking up for the first time, and eyeing her cousin with some sympathy, knowing only too well how it felt to be the center of such an attack. "And only the other day, all of the others were."

Joan looked at Elinor almost in fear, while her sisters and cousins looked uncomfortable with themselves.

Elinor sighed, weary of the entire conversation now, and desperate to be gone. "I need no apology, despite Partlowe's kindness to suggest it. May we please simply not discuss it any further, and leave my friends out of our conversations?"

"Yes," Joan immediately said, seizing upon the option with evident relief. "Yes, we may, absolutely."

"Excellent." Elinor rose, smiling just a little at the room. "If you'll all excuse me, I feel the need for a walk." She curtseyed, winked at Ellen, then strode from the room quickly, her steps filled with an agitation she couldn't properly express.

Oh, to be forced to spend more time in the company of people who thought so little of her! She'd never regretted her friendship with the Spinsters, though she had some regrets about her behavior within them. She had never found friends her own age with whom she had wished to associate closely, finding them to be silly and ignorant.

In the last year or so, she had found a couple of girls that defied that judgment, but she had only become friends with them because of the Spinsters.

She was who she was because of the Spinsters.

That was not going to change, no matter how her puffed-up cousins despaired.

Hugh's elegant speech and Partlowe's change of heart were not going to change the opinions of her relations, if only those opinions were discussed. It would be difficult to go on either way, knowing what she now did.

If she married, she would know that she surprised her cousins and they will have thought her cured of such an influence.

If she did not, the cloud of their cruel opinions and sickening pity would hang low over her at every family occasion.

"Damned if I do," she muttered as she walked further into the depths of Deilingh. "And damned if I don't."

"Oh, I'd be hard pressed to consider you damned no matter which way the wind blows."

Elinor stopped suddenly and looked around, unsure where the voice came from.

"Sorry," Hugh said as he stepped into the light provided by one of the sconces in the corridor. "I didn't mean to startle you."

"You didn't," Elinor managed, breathless yet again in the face of a man who had defended her so perfectly.

How could candlelight possibly improve a man who was already impeccable in looks in daylight?

More mysteries, more unanswered questions.

Less interest in finding the answers.

Hugh smiled and folded his arms, leaning against the wall. "And what, exactly, do you consider yourself damned about, Elinor?"

It was strange, she couldn't remember ever giving him permission to call her by her given name, but that, too, was mattering less and less. More than that, she loved hearing him say it.

Her name, his lips, his voice.

Perfection again.

A shiver raced down her spine, and she shook her head. "Oh, being a Spinster. Capital S," she added, seeing the question in his eyes. "After that, I'll never know if their opinions have changed if I marry or if I don't. They all want me to be more like Emma, who, as you know, was an unfortunate spinster, but then married for comfort rather than for anything silly such as romance."

Hugh was silent as he stood there, which was a blessing.

She did not wish for a commentary on the things she was about to reveal.

"The truth of the matter is," she told him with a sigh, "that I am afraid of being like Emma."

"Afraid?" he asked softly. "Of what?"

"Of settling for comfort as she did." Elinor swallowed and her fingers began to play together anxiously. "Not that Partlowe is a horrid man. On the contrary, he is rather good. He can be stuffy, pretentious, dull, and, until a moment ago, I didn't think he quite liked me, but he is rather good."

Hugh chuckled to himself, and it made her smile to hear it.

"Emma is happy, I suppose," she went on. Then she shook her head. "Well… content, perhaps. I don't know if that's enough for me. I don't need the grand sweeping romance that Charlotte is seeking and throwing away excellent candidates for, but I don't know that I could be happy with simple contentment, either. I shudder at the idea of a convenient marriage, especially if one might have a hope of something deeper and more sincere."

Elinor lifted a shoulder in a weak imitation of a shrug. "I thought that if I surrounded myself with women of similar ideals, I might benefit from their influence and find what I secretly sought. Instead, I find those women ostracized, and though I lack the same number of years, I feel the same ruthless banishment, even within my own family. I cannot give them up, as I have come to value them and their friendship beyond what I can express, but in declaring myself a Spinster with a capital S, I seem to have also declared myself the lowercase version, as well. And everybody in London agrees with it."

Hugh said nothing to this, the moment hanging heavily between them

She could not stand the awkwardness. She looked up at him with a bland, but playful smile. "Hence the application of the expression, you see."

He nodded in understanding. "I do see. Don't understand, but I see."

"You would have understood not all that long ago," she pointed out without malice. "Enthusiastically. When you were… a different man."

His eyes seemed to brighten, even in the diminished light around them. "You see it, then? The change?"

Elinor laughed quietly, the eager note in his voice giving her more joy than she should rightly have. "Of course, I see it, Hugh," she murmured, mirroring his pose against the wall. "I'd have to be blind not to."

His grin would have lit a ballroom with a brilliance beyond compare. "I cannot tell you what that means, Elinor. I cannot…" He shook his head, then cleared his throat. "I have hope, then."

"Hope?" she repeated. "Hope for what?"

"The future," he replied, his voice dipping, "and whatever it holds."

A tightness began in her chest, and rippled down the length of her, forcing her to push away from the wall and turn to continue walking, but not before turning to him, invitation in her expression, posture, and soul.

She didn't want to flee from him, only from her impulse to do something from which she could not retreat.

He took the hint and came with her, the two of them walking side by side, no particular direction in mind.

"So, what happened to Barbara and Mr. John?" Elinor asked, forcing her voice to be light.

Hugh chuckled with real delight. "Oh, they are in the library still. I have my recommendation for reading from her, but John required a bit more discussion. A voracious reader, that one. He'll need quite the list, I fear."

"Lord," Elinor laughed. "Must I rush to the library to ensure my cousin's virtue?"

"Not at all," he replied. "Your cousin Fredericka happened to appear after checking on her children, so they are quite suitably supervised. I think I could quite like Fredericka, if I knew her better."

"I like her myself," Elinor commented without hesitation. "She's a bit more pious than the rest of us, but that cannot exactly be faulted. Particularly at Christmas. And she has a great deal more sense than a lot of the others."

"And she is wed to… Mr. Tyson?" Hugh queried, wincing as he asked.

Elinor hummed in pleasure and nodded. "Very good, Mr. Sterling. They have three children, one of which is Phoebe."

"Ah, my favorite little friend." He chuckled and looked at Elinor. "She reminds me of you, you know."

Now it was Elinor who laughed. "Does she? I would have thought Amelia more like me."

Hugh made a soft sound of consideration. "You may have a point there."

Elinor jabbed her elbow hard into his side, making him stumble slightly even as his laughter continued.

"You suggested it," he reminded her. "I only agreed."

She rolled her eyes, shaking her head. "Impossible man. Not particularly gallant, are you?"

Hugh stopped and took her arm gently, but with enough pressure that she stopped as well. "Is that what you want, Elinor? Gallantry?"

Something in his words sent her heart skittering and swallowing became deuced tricky.

Still, she had to manage something.

"Sincerity," she half-whispered, meeting his eyes. "I don't need flattery or gallantry, or even chivalry if it comes down to it, though that would be nice."

"Find me a puddle," he murmured as his thumb began to gently rub against her arm. "I'll lay my coat across it for you."

That was oddly adorable, and she smiled at it. "There's no need," she told him. "After what you said in the drawing room in front of all my family? I have never seen or heard anything so glorious in my life, and I cannot see myself as worthy of it."

Hugh took a small step closer. "How could you not be?" he asked her, his look becoming something hot and intense.

Her cheeks flamed under such a look. "I raged against you, Hugh," she breathed, her eyes fixed on his. "I said… so many things. Unspeakable, vile things, all upon you and anyone that associated in the same circles as you. I cannot take any of them back, nor can I change to whom they might have been said. You are trying to restore yourself to a life you can be proud of, and the blame for any difficulties in doing so may be laid squarely at my feet and upon my shoulders."

"Elinor…"

She shook her head, swallowing hard. "I am so sorry, Hugh. I didn't know this man lay beneath that one. I was too proud and foolish to look."

He exhaled, his thumb still moving temptingly against her, the layers of fabric seeming to burn away under his touch. "I don't blame you," he whispered. "I fully earned every curse your lips could ever utter, and then some. You saw me for what I was, and I admire such honesty of sight."

"I should have been more generous with my opinions and thoughts," she countered, her fingers reaching out for the edge of his jacket, trembling with hesitation. "I should have been more like Izzy, or Prue, or Grace…"

Hugh's hand was suddenly at her cheek, silencing her at once. "I would not wish you to be anyone other than Elinor Asheley, madam. If you please. Is that understood?"

A pounding began in Elinor's ears, beating a steady cadence that drowned out everything else but the less steady breathing of her lungs. "Yes," she somehow heard herself whisper, not entirely sure what question she was answering.

He smiled a perfect, gentle smile at her, and his thumb stroked her heated cheek. "Good." He glanced up then, and his mouth curved with some amusement before his eyes were back on hers. "Your favorite plant, Elinor."

"What?" She looked and saw, ironically, a bunch of mistletoe hanging just above them.

Of course, it was.

"What do you mean by that, I wonder?" Hugh mused.

Her eyes fell back to his, her heartbeat picking up. "Did I say that out loud?"

He nodded slowly. "You did. I wonder what tone you wished those words to have."

His thumb caressed her cheek once more, and she shivered at it.

He seemed to laugh without actually laughing. "No one is here but us," he pointed out. "No one would know if you walked away."

Walked away? When the moment was so delicious?

She wet her lips, and Hugh's eyes darted there before slowly dragging back up to hers with new interest. "*You're* not walking away."

"No," he whispered, stepping closer. "No, I'm not."

They stood there, a breath apart, her skin only growing more heated beneath his touch, the moment suspended between them. Tradition dictated they kiss.

Her heart yearned to obey. Her lips tingled further still, waiting.

The kiss was there, hovering on the air.

All they had to do was…

Hugh slid the hand on her arm down until it reached her hand, cradling it in his own. Then he brought it up to his mouth, his lips caressing the back of her hand, her knuckles, and the base of her wrist, each one eliciting a further shiver that rippled across her skin.

He turned her hand over and pressed the gentlest of kisses to the burning palm of that hand, exhaling softly against the skin.

Oh, to burn in such a place and at such a time…

"Elinor?" the voice of Elizabeth drifted down to them. "Papa has asked that we sing again and requested I seek you out. Can you come?"

She was beyond singing anything at the moment, but she swallowed hard and sighed with some regret when Hugh brought her hand back down, holding it carefully in his own.

"Can I?" she asked him, though the question was a foolish one.

Hugh smiled and nodded. "I would like nothing better than to hear you sing again." He inhaled deeply, then released his breath and dropped his hand from her face, offering her a gallant arm.

Elinor stared at it for a moment, finding something quite sweet in such a gesture. She looped her arm in his, her now freed hand going to his upper arm and rubbing fondly.

"Then sing I shall, sir. Lead me on."

"With pleasure, Miss Asheley. With pleasure."

Chapter Eight

There is something quite magical in the air the closer one gets to Christmas day. One might even expect miracles, if so fortunate.

-The Spinster Chronicles, 17 December 1818

The Asheley family were undoubtedly welcoming curses of all sorts for trimming Deilingh with all the greenery and ribbons and anything that could be considered festive the day before Christmas Eve, rather than on Christmas Eve itself.

They had their reasons, their annual Yuletide Ball being the most significant one, so Hugh supposed they wouldn't be so very cursed.

Besides, what was a little curse among such boisterous and festive spirits?

Hugh rubbed his hands together as he paced the corridor just outside his room. He had been jittery all day, knowing what was to follow in the evening. After such a stunning evening and moment under that fortunately placed mistletoe, he had more hope than any man had a right to feel at one time.

Elinor Asheley was the beginning, center, and end of those hopes.

He had no set design, no speculation, not even a thought of what could possibly come from the ball tonight. After all, he'd attended several balls over the years with Elinor in attendance, and nothing extraordinary had happened at them. He'd been looking at Elinor for years without really seeing her and felt nothing at all in those moments.

Blind, blind fool.

But tonight… Tonight it could all be different.

He was seeing her now. And, if she were to be believed, she was seeing him.

It was strange; she was the first person from his past that he had connected with since he'd considered himself changed, and she had been the one that had terrified him most. Yet she had given him more joy and hope in the last few days than he felt he had a right to expect in his guilt and shame.

She had lightened him, and she was well aware of his burdens. She had made him laugh when he hadn't laughed in months. She had…

She had made him fall in love with her.

Lord above, was it possible?

He hadn't even been here a week, and now he was in love with someone he had known and despised for years. He couldn't deny it, the truth of the statement filled his heart and soul with glory. He loved her vibrancy and wit, her candor and her laugh, he loved the way her smile was slightly greater on her right side than left, that her eyes saw everything around her, and that she muttered under her breath no matter the circumstance.

She wanted sincerity in a man, she'd said.

Well, he was pretty bloody sincere at the moment, and when the moment was right, she would see that.

He loved her.

A wild laugh bubbled up within him, and he faintly pounded a fist against the wall with it.

Love.

So, this was what had turned his brother Francis into the man Hugh had considered to be a lovesick fool.

Lovesick his brother undoubtedly had been and was, but Hugh could no longer consider him a fool. Or, if he was, then they both were.

What a strange bond this was.

It was a pity Francis was not here now. Hugh desperately needed the advice of someone who had been through this mess, and it would help immensely if it was someone he could trust.

Francis would give him hell for it, but no more than Hugh deserved.

There would be time for that soon enough. If all went well, it would all happen quite soon.

For now, there was just tonight, and the Yuletide Ball.

Hugh patted the wall and pushed off of it, now striding to the stairs and practically dancing down them. Very faintly, he could hear the musicians beginning to tune, preparing for the guests and the dance. Supper would come later, and was destined to be excessive, as was everything else with this family, but he didn't mind that.

He was rather beginning to enjoy it, actually.

The musicians began to play a jaunty tune, and Hugh found himself whistling along as he entered the ballroom, pausing for a moment to appreciate the spectacle of the room. If Christmas could have decorated for its own ball, it had done so here. The room even seemed to smell of the festive greenery, mulled wine, Yule log… Every scent that could make one believe it was Christmas was alive in this room.

"Quite the sight, isn't it?"

Hugh turned with a smile to Elinor's father as he came beside him. "Indeed, Mr. Asheley. I can safely say I have never seen anything like it."

That seemed to please the man, and he looked around the room proudly. "A great compliment, that. We do try to do the thing properly at Christmas."

"It could hardly be more properly done, sir," Hugh assured him, "and I cannot thank you enough for welcoming me in and allowing me to experience it. I have not enjoyed a Christmas such as this in many, many years, and never quite like this."

Mr. Asheley turned and grasped him by the upper arms. "Not at all, my boy, not at all. You are most welcome, and it has been a pleasure to have you with us, to be sure. Always welcome at Christmas, and any time after this." He patted Hugh's arms and moved off to greet some arriving neighbors, all of whom appeared delighted to be there.

Hugh couldn't blame them. He was rather delighted himself.

He stayed off to one side of the room, watching as others entered and as some of the dancing began, though in small numbers.

Some of the cousins had trickled in and greeted him, and he remained tucked away, mostly to avoid Letitia, who was wild enough to try for any of the men, and had done.

As far as he knew, none of them felt likewise.

Then, in grand procession, came Mr. Asheley with his wife on his arm, and his children behind him. Mr. and Mrs. Partlowe followed first, then Edmund, Elinor, Elizabeth, and Ellen, the ladies all wearing some festive shade of red and bearing holly leaves in their hair.

Hugh could only stare at Elinor, her red and gold brocade perfectly embodying Christmas, the holly and gold ribbon wrapped around her exquisite golden hair seeming very much like a gift in itself. She glowed with her natural beauty, her cheeks tinged with a joyful blush that was only broken by her smile.

He had never seen anything so glorious, and it became difficult to swallow.

He didn't trust himself to go to her right away, preferring to let the ball officially open and the dancing commence as it would. She danced with her brother, with Dough, with two cousin husbands, and with some young man that made her smile far too much for his liking. He'd been mildly chastised by John Winthrop for scowling in a corner instead of actually enjoying the evening.

Winthrop had a valid point there, and Hugh could not deny it.

Would not.

The strains of a waltz began, and Hugh found his feet moving before he meant to, driving him towards the only woman he cared to dance with this evening.

She turned to him as he approached, and he prayed the light in her eyes when she saw him was not imagined.

He hoped it was not.

He bowed to her, then held out his hand. "Will you dance with me, Miss Asheley?"

Her hand was placed in his without hesitation, her fingers curving around his hand. "Yes, Mr. Sterling," she replied, smiling in a way that made him wish he could kiss her in this now crowded ballroom.

They moved out to the floor without a word, staring at each other, and he felt himself grow more breathless with every step. Now that he knew he was in love with her, the very sight of her was enough to render him thus. Pleasantly breathless, that was it.

Did he need to breathe, in all truth? It seemed an excessive action, all things considered.

The waltz commenced, his arm around her, her hand in his, the skirts of her gown continuously brushing against his legs. Each pass felt like the brush of skin to him, and it stirred his soul into something destined to drive him mad. They didn't speak; for his part, he could not.

Words failed him.

Holding her close as he was, there was nothing he could say. She was a vision, loveliness itself, and her perfect, full lips pressed into a small smile that curved with such charm he wanted to trace them with a finger. Her waist beneath his hand felt all too perfect, the dress perfectly molding to her impeccable form, and what skin was exposed seemed tinged with the same adorable blush that ever touched her cheeks.

Even in his mind, he was raving with compliments of her, flattery he could not speak, sincere though it was. She wouldn't wish to hear it, true though it was. And he would find a way to ruin whatever poetic phrasing he might have been able to prepare anyway.

Elinor had his full attention, and that was all he could do at this moment. Twirling with her, holding her, moving with her in this room, her natural citrus, cinnamon, and honey fragrance filling every one of his senses, he felt that everything in his world, in his life, was perfectly right.

He needed nothing else.

Need.

Oh, the word rose within him, repeated itself over and over in his mind, beat to the tune of the very waltz they danced to. He needed her, in ever so many ways. He needed her to make his life complete, to make his joy complete, to become the man he wished to be. Need for this woman and all that she could provide him.

Only her.

His grip on her hand tightened with the fervency of his wish, and the corners of her mouth spread a bit further, the barest hint of her teeth showing.

She looked as though she might laugh, and he so wished she would.

"Why do you smile like that, Elinor?" he asked, his own smile moving in response.

She hummed slightly. "I've never had a waltz such as this, Hugh."

"And that makes you laugh?"

"Yes," she replied simply. Then, of all blessed things, she sighed, and her smile grew further still. "Oh yes, it does. A perfect waltz must be enjoyed."

Perfect? Lord, but it was. It was perfection in a dance, but it was only perfect because of her, because love for her was going to burst his heart, because for the first time in a very long time, there was hope in his life.

She was his hope.

"Yes," he murmured, his hand gripping at her waist, his thumb absently grazing. "Yes, it surely must."

Elinor exhaled, seeming to shiver unsteadily as she did so, and he pulled her closer, mesmerized by the change he was witnessing in her fair eyes.

"Hugh…" she whispered, her lips barely moving.

They moved on a particularly large swell of music, and he felt his heart rise and fall with it. "Elinor."

Her lashes fluttered, and he knew he was lost. They were. Together.

He was not alone in this. He couldn't be. This moment was for both of them, the pair they had made, and the dance they were in.

No longer separate individuals, but moving as one.

Together.

The music stopped suddenly, and he blinked at the abrupt change, as if the moment was broken when the music stopped. As if only the music held that magic.

They stopped moving, and he looked into her eyes with as much regret as he could muster while still under the influence of so much joy. He found it reflected back, and with it, some of the magic.

All was not lost, then.

He smiled with promise, and Elinor looked away, tucking an invisible strand of hair behind her ear.

Her father stood by the musicians, his hands raised. "My friends, my friends, we have a most welcome surprise this year. Some rather pleasant locals have come and offered to sing us some songs, which I find to be most appropriate. So, if you will make some space for them, we will let our entertainment commence."

The guests moved, and Hugh and Elinor moved with them, shifting to one side of the room as simply, but warmly clad locals filed in, their cheeks bright with the cold.

Elizabeth hurried over to Elinor, her energy high. "Isn't this marvelous? They've never come before!"

Elinor released Hugh's arm and turned to her sister, the two of them whispering and giggling about something or other.

Hugh couldn't do so, as he suddenly felt the chill that these locals must have felt making their way from the village up to Deilingh. All because she had let him go. He cleared his throat, swallowing as he began a brief conversation he wouldn't remember with whomever was standing beside him.

A bell held by one of the villagers pealed once, which effectively silenced the gathering, then rang once more in the same almost haunting manner.

Then a tall man began to sing in a perfectly clear voice, no instrument to accompany him, his voice echoing in hallowed tones off the walls of the room. Another much lower voice joined his, and the two of them began to alternate phrases, the haunting bell pealing the slow cadence of the song.

A pleasant-looking woman began to sing then, followed by a girl who was clearly a daughter, singing in lower tones, just as the men had done. The joining of their voices gave the perfect tones usually only found in a church, and the gathering became something much more than a celebration of the season.

The four voices began to sing together, their melodies and harmonies changing hands with a skill that Hugh had never heard before in any gathering or performance. This was impeccable musicality, and the true joy and thrill of it could never be replicated by another group.

When the entire makeshift choir began to sing together, chills raced up and down his arms and his spine. His breath simply vanished from his lungs, and still no instrument accompanied the singers but the lone bell.

A timid, bare hand brushed against his once, then again, and he glanced over to see Elinor just as transfixed on the performance as he was, her breathing the slightest bit unsteady. She held a glove in one hand while the hand nearest him was bare. When she brushed against his hand once more, he captured it in his own. He watched as her breath caught, and her lashes fluttered as the quartet joined the rest of the voices in exquisite harmony.

Elinor turned her face towards him, and the same bewildered sensations he felt cascading across and through him were found in her expression. He slowly laced his fingers through hers, and barely breathed when her thumb began to move ever so gently against the skin of his hand.

Amazingly, the musicians began to join in with the singers, their brilliant tones adding and lifting to the glorious sounds already before them.

Hugh felt his spirit lighten and soar, as if it could have raised into the heavens itself on the wings of such a sound. He smiled with exhilaration at Elinor, and she returned it. They returned their attention to the exquisite music; the praises being sung seeming to him to perfectly fit the feeling of a particular thumb moving rather steadily against his suddenly tingling hand.

He could barely breathe for the wonder he felt with this song, with this feeling, with this love that would soon overpower him. The room seemed to be filled with angels joining their voices with these carolers, their power and purity equally matched by the mortals before them. He had never felt so moved by music in his life, and sharing the experience with the woman he loved, feeling her touch as a profound accompaniment, was joy beyond expression.

How would he ever go on after this?

The choir's voices began to fade, and with them the instruments. The initial quartet's voices were more clearly heard, echoing each other with soft precision, until only the first singer's voice remained, drawing out the last notes into the utter silence of the room.

As the music died away, Hugh felt rather as though applause would be inappropriate, far too common a thing for what they had just experienced. But applause filled the room anyway, though neither he nor Elinor did so.

They looked at each other instead, and he realized with a pang of agony that this connection between them, this moment, would shortly be broken. They would both go back to dancing at the ball without being able to be near each other. Not unless they wished to be open to comment, and he would not be able to hold her hand like this in public.

Elinor stared back at him, her expression pained.

He rubbed his thumb along her hand in a slow, deliberate stroke, and Elinor inhaled slowly, then exhaled the same, giving him a slight nod.

Hugh curved a lopsided smile at her and ran his thumb over hers once more.

She repeated the gesture, and he nearly declared his love right there and then.

Somehow, he managed to avoid doing so, a crowded ballroom of her relations not being entirely the right place for such a statement.

Reluctantly, he let her hand go, and she replaced her glove as the carolers commenced with a far more jubilant number, which prompted some of the more intrepid guests to return to dancing, though with the sort of feeling rarely found in Society. This was the rousing sort of dance the middle and lower classes usually enjoyed, and which Hugh had long secretly envied.

The guests not dancing clapped in time with the music, and Hugh noticed Elizabeth seeming to almost float with her enthusiasm as she watched.

He smiled to himself then took a step and turned to her. "Miss Elizabeth, would you like to join the dance?"

It was difficult to say whose smile was brighter, Elinor's or Elizabeth's. Elizabeth put her hand in his and nearly led him out into the dance, so delighted was she. The dance was energetic and spritely, and despite not being the partner he desired above all others, he would be hard pressed to find a dance in his memory that had been as much fun.

The rest of the evening was spent dancing with several of Elinor's other relations, though he did manage to avoid being snared into one with Letitia, which seemed a thing of mercy. His favorite of the night may have been dancing with Mrs. Asheley, Elinor's mother, who had seemed to appreciate the gesture a great deal. He had not danced with Elinor again, which had proved to be far more difficult than he'd planned, but his reasoning had been sound.

He could hardly promise that he would have been able to let her go if he had.

Saving himself had never been so agonizing.

But he had watched her, and it seemed that every time he had looked at her, she had looked at him. He lost count of the number of secret smiles they shared over the course of the night, but he could see each one in his mind's eye. A wondrous variety of smiles, and he adored each and every one.

Eventually, the ball came to a close, and the neighbors and guests left for their own homes, while the family returned to their bedchambers.

Hugh sat in his room for a bit but found himself far too agitated to even attempt to prepare for sleep. Despite the lateness of the hour, and the fatigue he felt seeping into his bones, he was not ready.

He paced his room for a bit, then decided a change of his surroundings would be better suited for it. He left his room, candlestick in hand, and quietly slipped from the bedrooms down to the main part of the house where he would be sure not to disturb anyone.

The gallery was his first destination, and he slowly ambled along the seemingly endless portraits of past inhabitants and relatives of the Asheleys, and even a few portraits of pets, oddly enough. He hid a yawn behind his hand, then moved back towards the now dark and empty ballroom.

Rather than enter, he leaned against the doorjamb, smiling fondly at the recent memories he had gained only hours before.

"So, you couldn't sleep, either?"

Hugh turned his head, smile already in place, to face the one person he most wanted to see in this moment.

Elinor.

She was still in her finery, though her hair had lost some of its perfection with time.

He liked it looser. Freer. More natural. More Elinor, in fact.

He would always be in favor of that.

"I don't know," he admitted softly. "I didn't try."

She laughed a little and came to stand before him, setting her candle on the floor near his. "Neither did I. The evening was too full of wonderful things, and I… Well, I didn't want it to end just yet."

Hugh smiled at his love. "Believe me, I perfectly comprehend the feeling."

Elinor smiled gently, rubbing her arms with bare hands. "You would, wouldn't you?"

He gave her a warm nod. "I would, indeed."

She said nothing to that, slowly rubbing her arms again as she looked into the ballroom. "Strange. It was so filled with light and music and joy not long ago, and now there is no hint there was anything there at all."

"Gone without a trace," he murmured, watching her instead of the room. "Only alive in memory."

"As with all the best things, it seems," Elinor replied. "No tangible hints to remember it by."

Hugh nodded, catching her whimsical meaning all too well. He leaned his head back and looked up, only to smile too broadly for the moment. "Well, perhaps an occasional tangible hint."

Elinor looked at him. "Oh?"

He only pointed up.

She looked, then grinned and began to laugh. "Ugh, it follows me."

Hugh straightened and stepped closer. "Can you blame the poor mistletoe? Why wouldn't it want to follow you?"

Elinor's smile faded, and she stilled. "I can give the mistletoe a list," she whispered, her eyes now trained on his.

He shook his head slowly. "Mistletoe doesn't need a list."

"No?" She took in a sharp breath and took a step towards him.

"Be careful," he warned. "We've been here before."

A small smile graced her lips. "Nothing happened."

"Well," he said with a soft gruffness, "mistletoe is quite dangerous, as we have learned, and more may occur than meets the eye."

"Really?" Elinor replied playfully. "Such as?

He shrugged. "Who can say? It might not be so easily defined. Dangerous thing, mistletoe."

"I'm well aware, Mr. Sterling," she informed him, a laugh in her voice, "and I'm not afraid."

"No…" he murmured. "No, you wouldn't be, would you?" He raised a hand and cupped her cheek tenderly. "Does anything scare you, Elinor Asheley?"

Elinor inhaled almost silently. "Yes…" she whispered, her voice trembling.

"Tell me."

"This." She brought her hands to his chest and slid them along the lapels, drawing with them the breath in his lungs. "This scares me, and I want it anyway."

Hugh swallowed once, already swaying towards her. "So do I," he breathed just before his lips touched hers.

She arched into the kiss, and his arm snaked around her waist in response. There was no hesitation on either side, tenderness and passion at war as their lips molded together, caressing and nipping, drinking from each other without reservation. She was sweetness itself even as her hands moved to grip his neck and his face with an eagerness that had him fairly laughing into the wondrous depths of her mouth.

He poured the very breath of life into this kiss, into this woman, professing all he felt or could ever feel in the truest form known to man. Her lips worked wonders against his, and the end of this kiss would surely end his life as he knew it.

His lips moved down her jaw, a soft kiss going to the base of her ear before he traced his way down the graceful column of her neck. Her fingers curled into his hair as he did so, and she cradled his head against her, bringing his lips more perfectly against her skin. Her shoulder received the faintest whisper of a kiss before she dragged him back for another foray of their joining lips.

Love, need, and desire joined into one as he kissed her, as she kissed him, and he knew his limits were fast approaching. He gentled his kisses, one hand moving to cradle her jaw so his thumb could stroke soothingly there as he tried to calm her, and himself.

Their lips parted, but hovered close as their brows touched. Their breath mingled in the confined space, panting unsteadily on both sides in the silence.

"I never knew," Elinor whispered as her hands slid back down to his chest. "I never even imagined, Hugh…"

He shook his head against her. "Nor did I, love." He kissed her lips softly. "Never."

She exhaled slowly, almost sagging against him. "What do we do now?"

Hugh chuckled and lifted his head, kissing her brow. "Now I think you had best go up to bed. I warned you mistletoe was dangerous."

Elinor hummed, her eyes narrowing. "I don't know. I found it all rather exciting."

"That's enough," he warned with a smile. "You need to go up to bed while you still can."

She giggled and laid a hand alongside his face. "And will you sleep, too?"

"I will," he vowed, taking her hand and pressing his lips into the palm. "And I anticipate very sweet dreams."

"One can hope," she said on a sigh. She winked at him, then stepped away. She picked up her candle, and gave him a coy, almost heated look. "Good night, Hugh Sterling."

Hugh bowed to her, casting her a wink as he did so. "Good night, Elinor Asheley."

Elinor nodded, hesitated, then moved away, laughing to herself in a way that made him grin outright.

"Merry Christmas, Hugh Sterling," he murmured to himself as he sank back against the door jamb, completely and delightfully exhausted. "Very merry indeed."

Chapter Nine

Upon reflection, perhaps in our lives there should be more reflection and less reaction.

-The Spinster Chronicles, 20 August 1818

"She's smiling."

"Of course, she's smiling. Why wouldn't she be smiling?"

"But she's… she's *smiling.* Not a usual smile, but… Just look at it!"

"I can see it, Elle. I'm not blind."

"E! Do something!"

Elinor glanced over at her younger sisters, still smiling the peculiar smile that was frightening her sister so. "Are you opposed to my smiling, Elle? Does it upset your breakfast?"

Ellen's expression was utterly comical. "No one should smile in that manner, at breakfast or any other meal."

Elinor looked at Elizabeth, who only rolled her eyes and returned her attention to the meal. "I'm done with the conversation, Elinor, but feel free to continue to engage her."

"Must I?" Elinor murmured, taking a bite out of her toast and chewing thoughtfully.

The three of them were in a parlor that had long been dubbed the Sister Parlor, and they were presently avoiding the melee of their extended family by taking their late breakfast together there. It was a pleasant, quaint room, the walls decorated with some of the drawings and paintings they had done over the years, though none had been truly masterful. Miniatures of each girl had been done at the age of fourteen, and those hung near the windows, though to this day, it was difficult to recall which portrait was of which girl.

Emma used to eat with them in here or retreat up to this room with them during particularly unbearable family moments they'd all wish to flee. She rarely came up here anymore, what with her husband and now the girls. There were simply too many other demands on her time.

Would the same happen to Elinor if she gained such a life?

No, she decided firmly as she took a sip of tea. She would ever be herself regardless of her situation. There was no reason why children could not come to this parlor and crawl upon the floor or sleep in bassinets or any other thing.

Any husband that Elinor would have would never object to such a thing.

She wasn't aware that she had stopped smiling at any point, and may not have done, but she smiled further at the thought.

"Oh, it's getting worse. I didn't think it could get worse."

Elizabeth choked softly on a bit of fruit, casting an amused look at Elinor.

Elinor looked at her youngest sister with a hint of a scold. "I am happy, Ellen. Why should I not smile if I am happy?"

"I do not object to your happiness," her sister insisted firmly. "Of course, I don't. But you are not a smiley person, sister dear. You never have been. Yet there you sit, all smiles and dazed looks, a sickening portrait of a woman of bliss, and I hardly recognize you. Must we have a discussion as to the cause of your smiles in order to return you to your natural state?"

Cautiously, Elinor took another bite of toast, wondering what she dare tell her younger sisters. The cause of her smiles was easy enough to identify, but how could she tell them that Hugh Sterling made her smile and laugh and dream, and that the heavenly experience of kissing him beneath the mistletoe had thrown her world on its head?

They might never believe her, and she had no explanation for the change in her.

No explanation for the waltz that had been the most evocative, romantic moment of her entire life.

No explanation for the breathlessness the touch of her fingers with his had caused.

No explanation for falling in love with the handsome, amusing, honest, and kind Hugh Sterling.

She paused, her teacup halfway to her lips.

Falling in love.

Love.

Good Lord, she was in love with Hugh Sterling!

Slowly she inhaled a shaky breath, then took the smallest sip of tea known to man before setting her cup down and exhaling in a rough *whoosh* of air.

"All right there?" Elizabeth murmured absently as she read a note she'd received.

"Yes," Elinor gasped as she dabbed her linen serviette at her mouth. "Yes, perfectly so." She cleared her throat and rose from her seat, almost fumbling for the edge of the table. "I find I am in need of a walk."

She left before either of them could make a reply, striding out into the corridor, one hand going to her brow.

How could she have missed this? How could it have happened in so short a time?

For pity's sake, she had been ready to throw him out on his pompous backside and run him over with a family carriage when he'd shown up at Deilingh just the other day! She would have lumped him in with the devil and his demons without blinking at it.

Now she was breathless with love for him?

But of course she was! The man had changed so miraculously, had proven himself a worthy heart and loving soul. He had seen the error of his ways and brought himself low into the fields of suffering to find the true nature of himself and to rid his character of the vile stains it had collected over time. He had sacrificed the life he had known and precious time with his family in order to seek redemption and restitution. He had pushed himself into the darkness in order to be worthy of, and to find more clearly, the light.

How could she not love a man who would go to such lengths to remedy his mistakes?

But more than that, she found in him a soul filled with goodness, humor, and strength. He had opened her eyes, and she hadn't known they were closed to begin with. It certainly helped that he was handsome, danced well, and seemed to know when she was ready to laugh, and joined her in it.

Elinor moved into the sitting room at the front of the house, settling herself in the window seat and tucking her feet under her as she looked about the room. This was the room where she had questioned Partlowe on the subject of mistletoe with the intention of making Hugh as uncomfortable as possible, or perhaps finding a way to turn the plant into a poison. He hadn't been intimidated in the least by it, and it had driven her to complete distraction.

She giggled to herself now, leaning her head against the wall as she reminisced. He was still driving her to complete distraction, but in very different ways.

There was no doubt in her mind that she did the same to him. She was, after all, quite opinionated, not to mention the fact that she had minimal talents for politeness. But Hugh didn't seem to mind all that much, which was promising indeed.

What was it that he had said? *I would wish you to be nothing more than Elinor Asheley.*

No one had ever wanted her to just be her, not even the Spinsters. Oh, her friends had certainly taken her as she was, but they tended to make a habit of shushing her louder opinions and dismissing her ideas. Perhaps that was only right, given that she had been a right tyrant in every way, taking the independence the Spinsters afforded and abusing it to the extreme.

She had grown since then. A changed Hugh had found a changed Elinor.

Perhaps their mutual changing had opened the doors to each other. Doors that would have remained closed otherwise, and they would never have known such joy was possible.

Was this the way it had been for all the rest? A sudden rush of realization that life would never be the same? That joy was more full and hope more complete? The impulse to smile that never seemed to fade and only grew with every thought of him?

What a wonderful, confusing muddle of things!

Hugh Sterling, of all people!

Charlotte would shriek to high heavens. The others would be reluctant, but relatively open-minded. After all, they had thought Camden Vale the epitome of improper at first, and now he was one of her favorites, if favorites were to be had. Once the ladies saw the man that Hugh was now, they would see that things were not as they once were.

The beauty of the way things stood now.

Oh, she needed to see him. She needed to be with him, walk with him, feel that breathless rush of exhilaration that only his presence could give her. She needed the chance to tell him, even if she might be too cowardly to do so straightaway. It might have been prudent to keep it as her secret for a time. There could be much good in letting herself relish in the knowledge and feelings and sensations of being near him and loving him, especially when he was unaware. It would add such an exciting, thrilling air to the thing.

What a right jolly Christmas this was all turning out to be!

Wild as she was to find him, she recollected the men had all gone out riding, as the morning had dawned rather fair, though it was still unusually cold. Glancing over at the clock on the mantle, she surmised that they ought to return shortly, and there would be a small window in which to speak with him in any privacy.

It was Christmas Eve, after all, and though the ballroom had been turned into the epitome of Christmas for the ball the night before, the rest of the house maintained the usual tradition of not being properly decorated as yet. That was the task of the day, and though Deilingh had servants aplenty to assist them, it was a long-held family tradition that all be involved in the project.

There were some adjustments to be made, especially once her cousin Lucinda had decided to take up a rare interest in cooking, and thus would spend the entire day in the kitchens with Mrs. Larpenteur, but, for the most part, the day was set before them. There would be light music and dancing this evening, and a relatively simple evening meal, given that the feast was to occur on the morrow. And, if tradition was kept, there would be a play put on.

An improvised pantomime, as it were. Of sorts, anyway.

They'd never been very good about such things. That, too, was tradition, and one of her favorites, actually.

The sound of voices brought her attention back around, and she rose quickly, grinning with excitement and hope. She moved quickly out the door of the room, brushing at her skirts and fussing at her hair in a sudden fit of nerves.

One should look her best when she's faced with the man she loves, once she knows that she loves him.

Surely, that was in the Spinster Chronicles somewhere.

If it was not, she would be sure to add it in the next article that she wrote.

She rounded the corner of the foyer, bright smile ready on her face, only to find Great-Aunt Julie and Great-Aunt Beatrice sitting in chairs and instructing a few footmen on the hanging of some greenery.

"No, no, you simple lad," Aunt Beatrice barked, thumping her walking stick against the floor. "What do you think it means when I say to your *left*?"

Aunt Julie squawked a laugh. "He *is* going left, you hussy. You mean to the right."

"Don't tell me what I mean, I know what I mean," Aunt Beatrice returned. "If I wanted him to go right, I would have told him so. Now, dear boy, if you will take that end to the left, please."

The poor footman, knowing what was really needed, moved the end of the bough to the right, and looked at Aunt Beatrice for confirmation.

"Exactly so, lad," came the pleased response. "Clearly, your handsome face is not all the quality you possess."

"Aunt!" Elinor protested as the footman's face heated.

The great-aunts looked at her without surprise or concern. "What?" Aunt Beatrice replied. "Should I not give him the compliment of honesty?"

Elinor covered her face with one hand. "Oh lord."

"Get that burly one we saw at breakfast," Aunt Julie requested of Sally, the head housemaid who was standing nearby for assistance. "I want him up on the ladder next. Best backside in the estate, and I am in desperate need of the view."

A fit of coughing began from the three footmen before them, and Elinor pointedly turned her face into the wall. "Saints and angels, kindly plead our case before the Lord so that the whole of the family is not judged for my aunt's eccentricities…"

"Oh, tush," Aunt Julie scoffed loudly, revealing the truth of her hearing abilities despite having spent years claiming to be deaf. "The Lord blesses the elderly with the freedom to speak as they will, and handsome servants with particular assets are evidence of his merciful benevolence to us."

"Are they indeed?" Elinor asked, turning her head to look at her aunts. "I had no idea."

Aunt Beatrice eyed her in return. "You seem flushed, Elinor. Are you quite well?"

Elinor nodded and turned fully, putting her back to the wall instead. "Quite well, thank you."

"Of course she's quite well, Bea," Aunt Julie blustered as she waved a hand in Elinor's direction. "The girl could hardly be otherwise when she's been kissed utterly senseless by that delicious Mr. Sterling."

Elinor fairly hiccupped with shock. "Pardon me?"

Her great-aunts cackled uproariously. "Oh, that was a good one, Jules!" Aunt Beatrice crowed. "A perfect dart, and right on the target!"

"I told you!" Aunt Julie insisted, holding out a hand. "I told you. A crown, if you please, sister."

"Gladly!" Aunt Beatrice reached into the pocket of her skirts and withdrew an aged reticule that jingled. She stuck her fingers in and pulled out a shiny coin and placed it rather delicately in her sister's palm. "Money well spent, and money well earned."

Elinor glared at them both. "I despair of you both, you know that?"

"We do," they said together with matching sage nods.

"And you're content with that?"

"Quite," Aunt Julie quipped, closing her fingers around the coin and waving her closed hand in the air. "Quite content."

Aunt Beatrice coughed into a lace handkerchief. "We'll die one of these days, you know, and then you'll all miss us very much."

"I'm sure we will," Elinor remarked dryly. She put a hand to her flushed cheeks. "That was uncalled for, you know."

"Most of what we say is uncalled for," Aunt Julie reminded her. "It's why we say it. Besides, love, you have nothing to be embarrassed about."

Elinor raised a brow at that. "Don't I?"

"'Course not," Aunt Beatrice retorted. "The man is a handsome devil, and cheeky enough to keep you on your toes. And so thoughtful. He even fetched us some punch last night, in lieu of our not dancing."

That made Elinor smile despite the ridiculous idea of her great-aunts dancing. "Sweet."

"He is," Aunt Julie agreed. "Kiss him some more, dear, and see if you can't get him to join the family."

There was no explaining or excusing her aunts, and she shook her head at them. But she had also learned some of her best moments of wit from them, and it was time to give it back to them.

"I shall do my best, aunt," Elinor replied as she pushed away from the wall and curtseyed. "But I make no promises. He may prefer a kiss from Letitia."

Her aunts immediately crossed themselves, and Aunt Julie took out a hidden flask and drank a swig. "Away with you, girl," Aunt Beatrice croaked with a laugh. "Save the man from that hag."

Elinor walked away, giggling to herself despite her embarrassment.

Charlotte would like her aunts. In fifty years, Charlotte might actually be just like them, and the idea was amusing as well as terrifying.

Elinor wandered the house a bit aimlessly, avoiding being dragged into any of the decorating that was already underway, for fear of somehow missing an opportunity to see and speak with Hugh.

Provided he ever actually returned to the house.

She was about to give up and return to the sister parlor or her bedchamber to mope in frustration when she heard the sound of male voices coming up from the kitchens.

They must have entered through that door rather than traipsing around from the stables! It made the most sense, certainly, and they were not so formal at Deilingh as to have a preferred door of entry.

What a silly thing that would have been!

Oh, Lord, she was rambling, even in her mind.

Calm. She must be calm.

She forced herself to inhale and exhale slowly, her hands going to her abdomen as she did so, the steady rise and fall of her body giving her something with which she could ground herself. She *had* to be grounded. Hugh would be appearing with members of her family, and if she appeared in the least bit overwrought, for whatever reason, they would call her out in front of him.

And that, she absolutely would not risk.

Could not.

The voices grew closer and closer, and Elinor tucked herself into the study nearest the door to the kitchens, remaining just inside so she might hear what the men might be discussing after their ride, and where they might go afterwards. She had to be strategic, after all.

"To break them up? What a feat that would have been!" her brother's voice said with a laugh. "A revolution, no?"

"Precisely," Hugh replied, his voice firm. "Something to give the men of London a chance. You wouldn't believe the influence the Spinsters have."

"Interfering busybodies the lot of them," an unfamiliar voice said in a tone she did not care for.

Elinor felt her hands become fists at her sides. *How dare they!*

"At any rate," Hugh went on, his voice drawing closer, "the attempt failed, and Tony up and married Georgie."

"Quite a disaster for you, wasn't it?" the same unfamiliar voice said with a laugh.

No, Elinor pleaded, pressing her back against the wall of the study in agony. *No, please.*

"It was indeed," Hugh replied, the door from the kitchens squeaking loudly as it opened. "So I set my sights elsewhere. Tried various other methods of ruination. Did you see a certain article earlier in the year raging against them?"

"I did," the other man said. "Quite well written, if a bit heated. Oh, that was you, was it?"

Elinor hissed through her teeth, her heart crashing through her stomach and nearly down to her toes.

"I wrote as I found," Hugh told him without much concern, or, apparently, regret. "If they could write so much against Society as a whole, why shouldn't I?"

"Ah, the power of the press," Edmund chuckled. "I understood that article was quite the topic of conversation in Society for some time."

Someone grunted.

"It ought to have been. It was meant to be inflammatory," Hugh said. "They deserved it."

They *what*?

No, this wasn't the man she had fallen in love with. This wasn't her darling Hugh, the one who had kissed her so passionately and with such adoration the night before. This wasn't the man who had waltzed her beyond her dreams and gave her wings to fly.

This was the reptile she hadn't thought about in days. This was the monster she'd fought so violently against in London.

This was the man she hated.

She squeezed her eyes shut, and found, to her surprise, a pair of tears leaking out from the corners and racing down her cheeks. She dashed them away at once. This was no time for that.

"Well, I cannot wait to tell Joan," Edmund chortled stupidly. "She'll never believe it."

"Tell her whatever you like," said Hugh. "It makes no difference to me."

Enough was enough, and Elinor could not bear one moment more. She wiped at her tears again and pushed off the wall, then strode out of the study, her hands still balled at her sides.

Her brother saw her first, and something in her expression must have warned him off, for he was quick to depart with whomever they had been walking with, abandoning Hugh to face Elinor alone.

Coward.

Hugh saw Elinor and broke out into the sort of smile that only a few minutes ago would have had her knees buckling. Now, it only fueled the ever-growing fire within her.

"How dare you," she ground out between clenched teeth.

His smile froze, then faded. "I beg your pardon?"

"I'm sure you do," she spat. She shook her head, words and emotions swirling in her mind, struggling to find their way into coherency. "I… I believed you."

Hugh's brow furrowed and he took a step towards her. "Believed me?"

She barked a harsh laugh. "You see? Even you cannot comprehend it. Why was I so foolish as to actually believe that you'd changed? That you could ever be anything but a snake in the grass."

It was as if she'd slapped him across the face, and she was quite tempted to do so, now she saw what that must have looked like. "What are you talking about, Elinor? I *have* changed. You know I have."

"Really?" She folded her arms, feeling as though she had just donned armor to stand her ground. "So you have changed, and yet the Spinsters deserved it?"

He shook his head slightly, confusion radiating from him. Then his eyes widened, and comprehension erased the lines of confusion. "Oh…"

"Yes, Mr. Sterling. Oh, indeed." She shuddered in revulsion. "I'd say I feel betrayed, but really, I feel more stupid than anything else."

"It isn't what you think," Hugh told her as he started to move in her direction.

She retreated at once. "Don't come near me," she ordered, her voice almost thundering off of Deilingh's walls. "Don't ever come near me again."

Something that looked like real pain seemed to enter his expression. "Elinor…"

Oh, he was a talented actor. Of course, he was. He'd fooled her, hadn't he? He had fooled all of them.

Elinor slowly shook her head. "Despicable. Does your villainy know any depth at all?"

"Let me explain, love," he pleaded, his voice harsh in its rawness.

"No," she snapped, holding out a hand as if she could force him away by will alone. "No, sir. You've said quite enough already. I'll thank you to never speak to me again, and to leave my family's home as soon as possible. And may the devil take you on the winter roads, Hugh Sterling."

She grabbed the edges of her skirts and marched away in perfect high dudgeon, feeling rather towering in majesty and righteous indignation. Aside from the strange crumbling sensation in her chest and the frantic pressing of her heart against her ribs, she felt perfectly right.

Tears began to stream again, but surely that was only due to high emotion.

Angry tears, surely.

Nothing else.

That was all.

Chapter Ten

Some things are said to be worth the winter cold. This author will remain skeptical unless such things prove themselves. Or we do.

-The Spinster Chronicles, 2 December 1819

It was astonishing that no one had forced her from her bedroom to participate in the Christmas Eve festivities. Her claim of a fearful headache must have been believed, which was remarkable, as Elinor rarely had even the slightest headaches.

Had they discussed her while she hid away in her room?

Had Hugh spread malicious rumors and lies to further his own ends?

That would have put quite the cap on his plans to end the Spinsters.

She shifted restlessly in her bed, tossing over, as she had been doing all night. Barely receiving a moment of sleep for the torment coursing through her, and even now, she didn't feel herself able to relax enough to rest at all.

The sky was beginning to lighten, she could see through her window, and it seemed pointless to pretend she would gain any respite. She sat up and pressed the heels of her hands into her eyes, sighing heavily.

It was Christmas morning, and she had never felt so ill on this day in her entire life.

She sniffled, surprised there were still tears anywhere within her, and rose from the bed, wearily moving to her bureau to find the most comfortable, drab morning dress she possessed, settling on a dull gray calico with long, thin stripes of black. Seemed rather apt for her current mood.

Silently, she dressed, putting on sturdy black slippers and grabbing a thick, burgundy shawl before slipping out of her room and down the seemingly endless corridor of family rooms.

Her footsteps were just as soundless as she wished; imagine having to face any member of her family after missing the entire night, not knowing if she was the topic of discussion. It would have been too much, and she undoubtedly would have found herself either dissolving into tears or lashing out in anger. Not particularly appropriate on Christmas Day, especially if they were to be attending the Christmas Day services.

"Elinor?"

She groaned and reached for a long tendril of her loose hair, running it through her hands over and over as she paused a step. She exhaled and glanced towards her sister, not bothering to hide how perturbed she was.

"Emma?"

Her sister stood there in her nightgown and wrap, one of the twins asleep in her arms. Emma gave her small smile, gentle in every respect. "May we talk?"

"I don't feel much like talking," Elinor admitted, though she moved towards her older sister anyway. "At all."

Emma swayed a little with her dozing daughter, nodding at her. "I can understand that, absolutely. But, if you can bear it, I would like to say a few things. All you need do is listen. Can you?"

So long as she was not about to be instructed, scolded, or insulted, she absolutely could listen to her. They had been rather close before Emma's marriage, and it would actually be rather wonderful to sit for a moment with her older sister, even if Elinor had nothing to say.

She nodded silently and stopped before her, leaning against the wall, reaching for her niece's pudgy hand.

"Yes. But only for a moment."

"That's all it will take," Emma assured her. She indicated her sitting room with a tilt of her head. "Shall we sit?"

They moved within and sat quietly, the clock in the room ticking almost ominously.

"I know what happened yesterday, Elinor," Emma announced in her gentle way.

Elinor flicked a humorless smile at her. "I thought you might. Nothing else to say to me, all things considered."

Emma gave her a look, clearly choosing not to comment on the statement. "Edmund told me everything."

Of course, he did.

"I've never been more disappointed in our brother," Elinor murmured, shaking her head. "He agreed with everything the blackguard said."

"Surely, you know Edmund better than that," Emma countered as she patted her daughter's back. "He adores the Spinsters; he finds it all a great laugh. He would never say anything against them."

Elinor scowled at that. She really did know it, knew Edmund was a bit of an idiot, but no villain. "So he was merely agreeing to avoid confrontation?"

Emma sighed as she shifted her hold on the baby, tossing her long plait over one shoulder. "Elinor, forgive my saying this, but are you really so prejudiced that you can't see the truth in front of your face?"

Elinor's jaw dropped and she gaped at her sister, feeling as though her side had been lanced with the accusation.

"Darling," her sister went on, her tone sympathetic, "Mr. Davis had asked Hugh Sterling how he had come across the Spinsters in the first place. Hugh was obliging him by relating the tale, every nasty piece of his involvement. He denied nothing and had nothing but praise for the Spinsters."

"I heard them," Elinor reminded her, wagging a finger. "He spoke of the article he wrote and said we deserved it."

"After which, he rolled his eyes and shook his head." Emma tucked a strand of hair out of her face and smiled at Elinor again. "He spoke of your influence with admiration, not grudgingly. And Mr. Davis is a sarcastic man, which you would know if you had spent any time around him. He doesn't think poorly of the Spinsters, either. He doesn't even know them, apart from the papers."

Elinor chewed on her lip, her sister's words having more an effect than she would have liked to admit. They chipped away at the walls she had thrown up the night before, and she felt those walls becoming rather unstable.

Emma rose gracefully, moving to open space to sway her suddenly fussing daughter. "Elinor, only moments before they entered the kitchen, Edmund says they spoke nothing but praise of the Spinsters, and of you in particular."

The walls crumbled and Elinor could only exhale a pained breath. "And Joan?" she asked, swallowing hard. "Edmund said he couldn't wait to tell Joan."

Emma smiled more broadly than she had yet. "He did tell Joan last night. He told her how violently Hugh had once felt against the Spinsters, and how he had changed since. Hugh said he didn't care, because he doesn't need anyone to understand why he feels the way he does now. He doesn't mind if the whole story comes out, because he is a different man now, and anyone could see that." Emma paused, then added, "And everyone does."

Elinor groaned and leaned forward, putting her face in her hands. How could she have been so foolish? She was smarter than this, wiser than to leap to extremes, and yet...

"I don't know what to believe," she whimpered, shaking her head. "I don't..."

"Edmund is a great many things," Emma interrupted, "but he is no liar. Never has been."

There was no arguing with that. Her brother was honest to a fault and was well known in the family for it. And he was also fiercely loyal to his sisters, which she had somehow forgotten the day before in all the mess of things.

If Hugh hadn't been raging against the Spinsters, somehow plotting a long-term strategy for their ruin, then he must have been true to the image he had given her of himself on this trip. That he was changed, that he was not the man he had been, that he admired her, and them, and...

And that he really was the man she loved.

"Oh, Emma," Elinor breathed, sliding her hands from her face to her mouth. "I should have known; I should have seen…" She shook her head and glanced at her older sister. "What did he do last evening?"

Emma smiled again, this time with sadness. "Well, he was rather downcast, but he was quite polite. He danced with Mama again, and she adored it. And he was so good with Ellen. You know how she can get ignored in our family parties, and it does rankle her so. Hugh was wonderful, and Ellen smiled the entire night."

Elinor grinned as she imagined the evening, her eyes burning with tears of joy and shame. "He would," she whispered. "He is very aware of the vulnerable ones. He even played with the children in the library the other day, and they adored him so."

She wiped away a stray tear that had fallen and shook her head.

"What?" Emma pressed. "Why shake your head?"

"I've ruined everything," Elinor said, her voice hitching in despair. "He'll never forgive me, not after I said I believed in his change, then went back on it."

Emma tsked in a motherly tone. "Do you really think a man who has worked so hard to redeem himself and to earn forgiveness would withhold it from others? If you think him so hypocritical, you don't deserve to love him."

The words sounded harsh, but Emma's voice lent them a softness that left only truth.

Truth.

Elinor *did* believe him. She *did* forgive him. She *did* love him.

And she needed to tell him. Now. Before all truly was ruined.

She was out of her chair in a moment. "I need to go, Em," she told her sister in a rush as she moved to the door.

"I thought you might," came the amused reply.

Elinor smiled to herself as she dashed down the corridor and down the stairs, knowing there was at least one other person who would be awake, and able to help her now. She had ordered Hugh to leave as soon as possible, and she had to know if any preparations had been made.

She hurried towards the study and exhaled in relief when the door was propped open, light within shining through the crack.

She knocked softly, but firmly, on the door.

"Come," her father's jolly voice called, missing the booming aspect it normally carried.

Elinor wouldn't think anything of that. It was, after all, still early in the morning, only just after sunrise.

She pushed the door open. "Papa?"

Her father was fairly casually dressed, sitting not behind his desk, but in his large and comfortable chair, a large book open in his lap. He smiled warmly as she entered.

"Elinor, my sweet. A merry Christmas to you, darling."

Elinor curtseyed in a fond show of deference. "Merry Christmas to you as well, Papa." Impulsively, she came over to him and pressed a kiss to his warm cheek.

In response, he patted her cheek and gave her a wink, the smell of pipe tobacco wafting into her senses. "You are up deuced early, my pet. It's long since you have been so eager for Christmas morning."

She blushed a little. "Not so, I always love Christmas, as you know."

He hummed in satisfaction. "Yes, I know. How is your head, dove? Better than last evening?"

"Much," she replied. "Perhaps excessive rest last evening left me eager to begin the day earlier than normal."

Her father nodded his agreement with the suggestion. "True enough, true enough."

The small talk was only heightening her anxieties, and she could not wait a moment longer. "Papa, may I ask you something?"

"Of course, pet."

She nodded once. "Have any preparations been made for the departure of our guests? It's just… I would hate for any of them to miss Christmas."

It was a weak excuse, but her father did not seem to notice. His expression soured and he nodded, causing her heart to sink. "Yes, unfortunately. Mr. Sterling is leaving momentarily. He's just taken his leave of me, come to think. Graciousness itself, he was, but said he must make his way to his own family." He shook his head, suddenly appearing almost grumpy. "Wouldn't even stay for Christmas breakfast."

"He… he's leaving?" Elinor gasped, clutching at her shawl in distress.

Her father nodded moodily. "He said the roads were in much better condition, though I don't know where he got that information, and said he felt he ought to make an earlier start."

No… No, he couldn't…

Elinor stood there for a moment, frozen in shock, and then, without a word to her father, she tore from the room at a sprint.

All was prepared now, and he just had to mount the horse and ride away.

It was safer to take the horse than attempt the roads with the carriage again. He had given Mr. Asheley the impression that the roads were much clearer, but, in all truth, he was just desperate to leave.

Elinor wanted him to leave.

How had a place that had filled him with so much hope so recently filled him with equal despair? If not more despair, given his current state.

He rubbed the nose of the horse he was borrowing, clicking softly as the animal panted in the cold morning, its breath creating clouds of fog spiraling into the sky.

"Easy, lad," he murmured, smiling without emotion. "It's only a quick ride. We'll meet up with the coach as soon as the roads are clear enough, and then you'll have a warm stable until the groom can fetch you back."

The horse snuffled in response, nudging against his hand.

Hugh chuckled and scratched the horse fondly. "You'll take me for quite the ride, yes? We might race a bit, if the path is clear enough."

There was no response to that, and Hugh patted the horse again before moving to adjust the saddle and see to the few belongings he was bringing with him.

He paused, breathing slowly as he truly considered leaving Deilingh.

Leaving Elinor.

The change in her had broken him. If she could change her mind about him, so would everyone else. He would have no hope of true reconciliation, as everyone would suspect his claims to be feeble, and that his true nature was the one he had previously shown.

His family would welcome him back, of that he was certain, but beyond them, he had no confidence. What if his letters of apology were refuted by those he had sent them to? What if his redemption was not complete, and he had more to atone for?

He would make amends with his family, and then he would retreat again. Reduce himself into obscurity until he felt himself changed enough to venture out once more. Until he could be believed, in all sincerity.

Until his change was genuine.

The devil of it was, he'd thought it was.

Until Elinor.

The woman he loved did not believe him. Did not believe *in* him.

Did not see the man he was now as different from the man he had been.

What was the point of anything if that was true?

Hugh shook his head and nodded at the groom who had come out to assist him. The man bowed in response, then turned back for the stables, rubbing his hands together in the cold.

Alone entirely, Hugh looked back at Deilingh, the place he had begun to think of as perfectly ideal.

It pained him to leave it. To leave the family. He hadn't truly been part of a family in some time. This place, and her family, had restored him to it. But only for a time, and now that was over.

He pulled his greatcoat more tightly around him, patted his scarf, and nodded to himself. He hoisted himself up into the saddle and tightened his heels against the horse.

"Ready, my friend?" he murmured, leaning down to pat the horse's neck as it began to shuffle in agitation beneath him. "All right, then."

"Wait!" a light voice called in the winter morning air.

Hugh stilled, his breath catching. He exhaled, watched the fog of it curl away, and waited.

"Wait!" the blessed voice called again.

There was no mistaking it now, and he turned towards it.

Elinor was hurrying down the path from the front of Deilingh towards him, deep red shawl wrapped around her, gray skirts flapping with the swift motions of her legs. Her long, fair hair bounced loosely around her shoulders, dancing to and fro with her haste.

He had never seen anything more lovely in his entire life.

"Careful!" he called out in warning, unable to help himself. "The path is icy."

She flashed a quick smile and eased her pace only slightly, her steps becoming more careful, but with no less energy.

Hugh drank in the sight of her as she neared him, loving how bright her cheeks were, either from cold or exertion. Loving how her hair naturally curled only at the ends. Loving...

Her. Just loving her.

His heart ached, tightening within him when she finally reached him.

"Hugh," she panted, out of breath. She gripped the horse's bridle as if by her power alone she could hold him there. "Thank you for waiting."

He could only nod for a moment. Swallowing, he managed to add, "Of course."

He wasn't sure what he meant by that. Of course he would have waited? Of course he didn't mind? Of course he would do anything she asked?

Of course was the proper answer to all of the above, and to several more questions she had but to ask of him.

If only she would.

Elinor looked up at him, her eyes luminous in the morning light, amidst the white of the surrounding snow and frost-covered trees. "Oh, Hugh..."

That tone... Heavens, he would have gathered her in his arms for a moment with that tone, if only he felt able to.

"What?" he asked, almost pleading for her to get on with it. He had no notion of what to expect from this, and he feared the pain it might bring just as he feared the hope now pressing on him.

"I'm sorry," Elinor said, a slight catch in her voice. "I am so very sorry. What I said yesterday… It was not fair to say, and I didn't mean it."

He stared at her, hardly breathing, barely blinking. "Which part of it?" he asked her, wary and hesitant.

She seemed to be relieved at his response, but he couldn't understand why. Perhaps it was the same reason he was beginning to feel it.

They were speaking to each other, and that seemed its own kind of miracle.

"Any of it, honestly." She shook her head, the hand on the bridle moving to the horse while the other clutched at her shawl more tightly. "It was unforgivable. I fell victim to the trap you warned me about; I saw who you were instead of who you are. I assumed the worst based on the small part I heard and would not listen to the truth."

Her throat worked on a swallow, and he watched that delicate throat move, captivated.

Elinor moved her hand along the horse a little, towards him. "I see the change in you, Hugh, and I know the difference."

A wondrous lightness began to fill him, and he smiled with the joy of it. But that joy was short-lived, as was the smile. Pain wedged itself in, and despair wrapped itself around him.

"But is it enough, Elinor?" he asked as the agony within his chest began to tighten his throat. "Will it ever be enough?"

Somehow, the woman he loved smiled with tenderness as well as an air of mischief.

"I certainly hope so," she quipped softly. "I've run all the way out here in the snow without a proper coat or boots to tell you that I love you and beg you to marry me."

All sensation and thought fled from him, and he could only stare at her as his heart, or what had once been his heart, began to pound in a fervent but unsteady rhythm.

"I beg your pardon?"

"You have my pardon," she informed him, moving closer, "and my person, if you want it. I'm in love with you, and I want you to marry me."

He laughed a faint, breathless, nigh delirious laugh. "And you came out into the snow for this?"

Her hand rested on his boot, and somehow every single one of his toes felt the warmth of her skin. "I couldn't let you get away. You may be my only chance, and I know I will never love like this again. So…" She paused, swallowing again, "Will you?"

Was she mad? The answer should have been as plain as the sun now rising above them. "Yes," he insisted. "Yes, of course. I loved you the moment you threw your mistletoe at me, and I knew I couldn't hope… Come up here."

He reached a hand down, and she took it, placing her foot atop his and letting him pull her onto the saddle with him. It was in no way comfortable, but he knew she wouldn't care. He opened his greatcoat and wrapped it around them both, encircling her with his arms.

Elinor touched his face, and one tear hovered on her cheek.

He kissed that tear, then found his lips pressing against hers, with hers caressing his in return. Her arms slid around him, beneath the folds of his coat, her hands pressing into his shirt, as though they could reach beneath his skin as well. There was no haste to this kiss, no frantic energy, just a deep, fervent intent that stole every thought and breath.

Nothing else in the world existed but them, and this kiss, this connection. There was no other sensation but her lips and her body against his, the feel of her hair against his fingers.

There was no telling how long they kissed, all sense of time and space vanished with it. It faded into a series of softer, grazing kisses, nuzzling that warmed them both until the winter cold had no power whatsoever.

"Merry Christmas, my love," Hugh rasped against her lips, the words making the tender flesh hum between them.

Elinor sighed and pressed her lips to his for a moment. "Merry Christmas," she eventually replied. She pulled back and brushed his hair away from his face, his hat having vacated its position at some point. "Will you come back to Deilingh, now? I want to spend Christmas with my intended."

He chuckled and brushed his nose against hers. "I can agree to that," he murmured, pulling her closer still. Then he hissed as one of her hands reached for his face again. "Ooh, darling, you're freezing. You shouldn't have sacrificed your toes for me."

She gave him a rather pointed look. "You weren't supposed to leave this soon, so I was unprepared!"

Hugh shook his head and reached for the reins around her, turning the horse back to the house. "Next Christmas, I am getting you a sturdy pair of boots to keep on hand."

Elinor huffed indignantly even as her arms tightened around him as they rode. "Why not this Christmas?" she demanded. "We are engaged, after all."

"Well, I wasn't planning that far ahead when I was stranded…" he tried to explain.

Elinor rolled her eyes dramatically, making him chuckle. "A likely excuse, Hugh Sterling. What in the world am I going to do with you?"

"I have an idea about that, actually." He pulled the horse to a stop and held up a finger, reaching into the pocket of his waistcoat.

She watched and waited, a wry smile playing at her perfect lips.

He pulled out the small bough of mistletoe and dangled it above their heads. "Look familiar?"

Elinor giggled as she looked up at it, her arms slowly stroking along his back. "I do believe that is the exact mistletoe that came flying at your head not so long ago."

"Indeed it is, my love," he replied, leaning closer. "I've been told the only way to break the curse of having mistletoe thrown at you is to spend a lovely amount of time obeying the custom beneath it."

"Really?" she purred as she bumped her nose against his. "What wise individual imparted that bit of wisdom?"

Hugh quirked his brows at her, grinning. "Partlowe."

Elinor's eyes widened, and then she burst out laughing, one of her hands coming up to slap his chest. "Stop that, no he did not!"

"Letitia?" he suggested next.

Her giggles overcame her, and she dropped her head to his shoulder. "No. No, absolutely not."

Hugh kissed her head, smiling still when she raised up to look at him once more. He stroked her cheek and her bottom lip. "Would you believe Uncle Dough?"

Elinor sighed and nuzzled him. "Probably. But let's not make a habit of mentioning Uncle Dough before you kiss me."

Hugh chuckled and briefly caught the lips of the woman he adored with his own. "I can agree to that, my love. Now, beneath this mistletoe, will you kiss me again?"

She hummed a smile against his lips. "Of course, my love. Always."

Then they kissed again, and for quite some time, until any and all curses were gone.

Epilogue

The workings of fate are oft times bewildering, befuddling, and beyond understanding, be you spinster, bachelor, spouse, or spawn. No one understands fate, and no one is safe from it.

-The Spinster Chronicles, 30 December 1815

"Unbelievable. Absolutely unbelievable."

"What is?"

"I am astonished. Astonished, I tell you."

"Congratulations. Care to share?"

"Apparently, if someone wants to get a husband, they just needed to accompany Elinor to her family's estate for Christmas!"

Lady Edith Leveson sat up straighter and looked at Charlotte Wright in abject confusion. "What are you havering on about, lass?"

Charlotte waved the letter she was reading in the air, her eyes widening with impatience. "I have a letter here from Elinor. She's to be married!"

Edith blinked unsteadily, waiting for her friend to laugh after such a fine joke, but the utter disdain in the woman's face told her that laughter was not to come. "Crivvens," she whispered. "Truly?"

"Would I make something of this severity up?" Charlotte demanded.

"Well, I dinna ken if you're aware, lass," Edith said with some impatience, "but you can be a wee bit on the dramatic side."

That earned her a raw glare, but Charlotte returned to the letter with a huff of some offense. " 'You'll hardly countenance this'," she read in a stiff tone, "which she got right, 'but I am to be married. It will take too long to describe in this letter, but the man to be my husband is Hugh Sterling.'" Charlotte snarled like a rabid dog. "The very idea. What nerve, the idiot girl. 'He is much changed, and I cannot wait for you to know and accept him as I do.' Not bloody likely."

Edith sighed and shook her head as she sipped a rapidly cooling cup of tea. "Is there any chance of getting the information without having the additional commentary?"

Charlotte huffed even louder at the request. "You're a peculiar friend, Lady Edith, and I'm not sure I appreciate it."

"Alas, I'm the only one ye've got at the present," Edith replied without concern. "The letter, if you please."

"Very well," came the dry response. "Let's see here… Hmm…. oh, here. 'As luck would have it, our engagement was not the only one that took place at Deilingh this Christmas. My cousin Barbara is to wed Mr. John Winthrop, brother to Lord Winthrop, and my disagreeable and desperate cousin Letitia has consented to wed my father's cousin's son, Rupert Perry, which we all find to be a dreadful idea.' Well, at least it's a husband, so well done, Letitia, I say."

Edith grunted without commitment, disagreeing heartily, but deciding not to go into that. Everyone knew that her marriage had been unhappy, though no one on the earth knew the reasons behind it. It was best that those details remained secret.

For now.

"Oh, and Janet Sterling had her baby!" Charlotte exclaimed, sounding much more delighted by this topic.

"Was she up at Deilingh, as well?" Edith asked, bewildered at the idea.

Charlotte gave her an incredulous look. "Of course not, I've only just remembered it. Why in the world would Janet Sterling be at Elinor's family estate during her confinement?"

"I dinna ken, Charlotte," Edith sighed heavily, sinking back against the couch. "Tha's why I asked ye. What else does Elinor have to say?"

"Well, she invites us to the wedding, but I highly doubt I can attend." Charlotte sniffed as she refolded the letter and set it down, reaching for a biscuit.

Edith eyed her friend with amusement. "Why ever not? Do you have a more pressing engagement?"

Charlotte looked at her, biting hard into the biscuit, her dark eyes flashing. "No, but I am certain I could find one. I highly doubt Mrs. Asheley would look kindly upon me spitting at the groom during the service."

"I would concur with that." Edith snickered softly, shaking her head. "Charlotte Wright, you're a rare one."

"So I've heard," she replied, breaking a smile for the first time in minutes.

Edith sighed and closed her eyes, resting in the comfort of Charlotte's parlor. "Well, I suppose Elinor must know what she's about. She hated Hugh Sterling more'n you did, so if she can marry him…"

"He probably compromised her."

That earned Charlotte a throw pillow to the head, even as Edith laughed about the idea. "She'd have torn his limbs from his body had he tried any such thing, and ye ken it well!"

"I know, I know," Charlotte moaned as she propped the pillow behind her head. "It's only distressing that Elinor Asheley has found herself what she considers to be a suitable match before I have."

"Aye, I can see how that would trouble you," Edith allowed, "but, in all fairness, lass, I dinna think you've really looked all that hard."

Charlotte looked rather defiant for a moment, then slumped back in defeat. "Perhaps not. It's all become a bit of a farce now. A game I play to amuse myself amid the tedium."

Edith heard true notes of sadness in her friend's voice and smiled with some sympathy. "I canna speak for all marriages, as ye well ken, but I believe that for the best marriages, you have to be willing to give of yourself in some way. Are you prepared to do that for any man?"

The thought seemed to strike Charlotte, and she looked quite pensive for a moment. "I don't know," came the hesitant response. "It never occurred to me that that would be how it should go."

"Nor I," Edith murmured, memories racing through her brain

with painful clarity. "But it is worth considering."

"Hmm," was all that Charlotte said.

Nothing else was said for a moment, and Edith felt herself relax in the solitude.

"I'll consider it some other time," Charlotte said with a sleepy yawn. "Right now, I only want a respite and to dream of tripping Hugh Sterling as he walks to the front of the church on his wedding day."

Edith snickered again as she pictured the scene Charlotte described. "That would be a sight to behold."

"It would indeed."

The picture of Elinor's wedding shifted, morphed, and turned into another wedding day; one with far less amusement.

Faces flashed in her mind, all bearing the same look of resignation. She heard someone crying, but she couldn't find the source of the tears. A veil fell before her face, faded lace that was yellowed with age, and the sounds of tears grew ever louder.

She was moving, gliding up the aisle, even as she tried to turn back.

She couldn't do so, couldn't move. Her arm was held fast, and she was dragged forward.

"Ye're not getting awee," her father's gravelly voice growled in her ear. "Succumb, and say 'I do', an' we can all get along wi' our lives."

"Please," she heard herself whisper. "Please."

Her arm was released, and she was suddenly before a man, though she could not see him clearly.

No, her mind cried out. *No, please.*

Her veil was raised, and she faced the man to whom she would be wed.

His eyes met hers, and he smiled, turning her blood cold.

Edith jerked awake with a panicked gasp, though she was not entirely sure she'd been asleep. She dabbed the back of her hand to her brow, wet her lips, and rose from the couch.

"Charlotte, lass, if yer no' needing me, I think I must be off. I'll call upon you tomorrow."

Charlotte nodded even as she nestled further into the confines of the couch. "Forgive me for not bidding you farewell."

"Of course," Edith murmured with a smile her friend would not see.

Edith turned from the room and quietly gathered her things from the maid while her carriage was brought round.

She could not keep doing this, she thought as she loaded herself into the carriage. She could not live trapped in her memories and unable to move in her present, only to fear the future.

She would not.

Edith closed her eyes and leaned back roughly against the worn seats of the barely usable carriage. Something would have to change, and it would have to change now.

Or it never would.

Coming Soon

What A Spinster Wants

The Spinster Chronicles
Book Six

"A spinster by any other name."

by

REBECCA CONNOLLY

CPSIA information can be obtained
at www.ICGtesting.com
Printed in the USA
LVHW030827110320
649571LV00003B/43

9 781943 048984